THE RARE FLOWER

THE RARE FLOWER

Adrita Hazra

KALPAZ

ISBN : 978-93-5128-060-6

Price : ₹ 190

First Published, 2014

Published by

Kalpaz Publications
C-30, Satyawati Nagar,
Delhi-110052
Ph. : 9212142040
E-mail: kalpaz@hotmail.com

Laser Typesetting: Gyan Print, Delhi
Printed at: Chawla Offset, Delhi

Cataloging in Publication Data--DK
Courtesy: D.K. Agencies (P) Ltd. <docinfo@dkagencies.com>

Hazra, Adrita.
The rare flower / Adrita Hazra.
p. cm.
Novel.
ISBN 9789351280606

1. Love stories, Indic (English). 2. Indic fiction (English). I. Title.

DDC 823.92 23

Preface

'True love', the moment you hear these magical words, the sweetest of imaginations start conjuring up in your mind. Love must have been the first word that was felt, understood and expressed by humans. And why only humans? Even animals give us some wonderful glimpses of love and care. Love is a state of the heart and no matter how many definitions you try; you will always feel exhilarated and blessed once you are in love. Even with closed eyes, you can feel its presence and your heart will keep dancing to the melody of its beats. The intensity experienced during love is truly expressable. Sharing love stories makes us remember and feel the eternal love and it completely redefines the way one experiences love.

The story of Varun and Aisha is touching but tragic. We were friends, the kind of friends who could be called as the best of friends. We studied together, sat in together and even ate together on occasions. Misunderstandings -Well! We did share a special chemistry.

She was sincere, smart and beautiful; God bestowed her with everything a girl would desire. While I was just a naive and an immature kiddo, a simple employee in a bank and she is the boss in her company (Though she has her own firm).

Sitting by her side, I could not find anything more important to do other than adoring her. She didn't notice it, and even if she noticed it, she didn't give it much attention. We met in Gwalior. She was just the opposite to the kind of girl whom I would want to fall in love with. She was from a rich family with lots of expensive branded clothes and infinite number of sandals and I was from a middle class family with just a pair of jeans, some full shirts and one pair of slippers. She had travelled the world while I had never even travelled domestically by an aeroplane; her one time shopping expenditure would be equivalent to my yearly shopping budget. We were completely different.

We became friends in a few months. We used to study together, dine together, talk late nights and discuss each and every detail of our life with each other. We shared everything, from silly jokes to the most serious issues of our lives and then laugh on it as if nothing happened.

But something happened in a month when Varun and Aisha's life turned upside down!

Adrita Hazra

Acknowledgement

To all those people who change and to those who don't!

THE RARE FLOWER

It was 7 O' clock in the evening of April 13. The night has fallen in the small city known as Gwalior. I am on the highway Café house as usual I am on the same coffee table as of the basic brand Angela's Coffee shop. Some people call it a Coffee place; I call it a little corner of paradise. It was just three years ago, my friend walked me down to Angela's for my first taste of COFFEE. Since that day, whenever I want Coffee, I always think of Angela's coffee. In fact, coffee just isn't coffee for me unless I'm having it amid the sight and smell of Angela's. On the outside, there's an ancient neon sign that buzzes and flickers against the peeling white paint on the rough brick wall. Inside, is an antique espresso machine that sits like a brass robot guarding the front door. Angela' stables are topped with red and white linoleum patterned to look like old-fashioned checkered table cloths. Imitation Tiffany lamps hang over each table and send multi-coloured flecks of light dancing across the room and along the painted Indian street scenes. Angela's has lots of "regulars" for whom the restaurant is a part of their lives. League teams go in to celebrate victories or to ease defeats. A group of white-haired men meet at Angela's every Friday; they sip their espresso and talk about politics and sports in a mixture of Hindi and English. Young couples usually occupy the quiet corner tables for two. I turn the slightly greasy door knob to open Angela's front door, the first thing that greets me is a wonderful warm cloud of enticing Coffee scent. I am at my table lighting my cigarette and placing it between my lips and throwing smoke in the air on the lounge waiting for my date to come. She was my fifth date (5th girl) in this month.

So, as she is the fifth girl in this month you would have recognised that I am a kind of guy who can never be serious with any kind of girl. Yep, I am a player. I grew up in Calcutta and studied in Delhi for a few years and now I have shifted to Gwalior for the past three years. Three years and 50 and odd dates. The evening was the same as usual but a little cooler with a cool breeze touching my face. The sky was so dark, it was as if someone had thrown a moth-eaten blanket above earth, and the stars were the little holes that had been eaten away by the insects. The ashes on the ashtray were increasing with every cigarette of mine between my lips, I was going through my blackberry black phone and I heard an unusual noise of music which was insanely different and a series of honking noises of horns, the music playing in the car was very loud as it was audible "DON'T STOP N MOVE".

It was loud and was on the top of all the noises and was clenching the ears. A yellow car with the accelerator pushed to the most. The Yellow Figocar that had hit the road at its peak speed must be running at a speed of at least 100 km/hour or more. Honking the cars' horn like an impatient creature. The car stopped, I went back to look at my phone. I was texting and suddenly my eyes froze at the car. I could see a white skin figure with flat bellies which were also in yellow colour, wearing a lovely blue dress that was just above the knee teamed with a thin black belt that made her look more attractive. It was complimenting her sexy figure. This is a young woman, probably about twenty years old, who stands with an air of carefree confidence that is most noticeable in her serene blue eyes outlined with a dash of kohl. Soft face with rounded cheek bones, proportionally slim and sharp nose, high non-trimmed brows, soft pouty pink lips, and the rounded chin is complimented by her easy, charming smile. Though, there is a hint of a wild spark lingering behind those lids. She adorns jet black hair, groomed and shining brilliantly, which crops her gentle face; the mane glimmers down to her waist where it ends, with perfectly cut tips. The uniform hair spills down between her shoulders blades in a bladed formation, the rest of it cropping in circular fashion towards her shoulders where the shortest strands just barely tickle the skin of her collar bone. This young woman has a soft neck and narrow shoulders that form into equally lithe arms and hands, but her mid-section shouldn't go without noticing. Overall her general shape is a toned, hourglass figure defining her chest and hips which are of moderate, if not of winding 'definition'. Altogether her skin tone is a light and even a bit fair lending her to aporcelain glamour. She is a feathery woman, but owns many womanly curves that are upheld with a firm youth that bargains the opinion she is, again, probably in her early twenties.

Long straight black hair which were ending till her waist. She stopped just a little near from my coffee table of the lounge. With a cute charming face which was serious with wondrous oceans of blue, gaze out in playful curiosity as she smiled. When she found a small black puppy on the road, she hugged it and its tails was wagging at about a million miles per hour (even if the tail is just a stub) as it saw her… A happy puppy is ready to play with anything and will chew on everything. She picked it up from the road and took it with her. That cute look, I have ever seen in my life. That INNOCENCE at its peak I have seen girls pretty, hot, beautiful but she was totally different and totally unique. I was watching her with my full soul because I have never seen such innocence and she must be in her early 20's and she was beautiful. I was looking at her as she picked up the black pup and started to walk away and. . . . . .

Hey Varun! - A girl said

Here was my date. She came in front of me and all I could see was the yellow ford Figo hooping by! 9

My date came and I cannot tell you the details of what she was wearing because it only lasted for about thirty minutes as I was enjoying and I wanted to see her as to where did she rush away. And when the night came the enhanced glamour that belonged not to my date or to the cool breeze it belonged to the yellow Bellies girl.

I was on my way home, almost reaching home and I saw the same the yellow belly girl entering into a house which was just next to me, She was entering the Roy Mansion but I haven't seen her before in these three years. She was parking her yellow Figo in the house. I peeped into the car when she was trying to park.

There was the black pup which was the same which she picked up near Angela's. It was wearing a seat belt sitting on the front seat (HA ! HA! HA!) . She looked up at me and turned off immediately as if I never existed.

I was just about to give her a smile but before I could she was already into her house. I was hypnotised or what? Its 10:30 pm. Ma is gonna kill me! By the way my name is Varun and I am the narrator!

It was 11:00 am and I was very late for office, I was struggling with my files and folders and managing to put them in my black leather bag quickly and was rushing towards the main gate of my house. My house was a simple house painted with beige colour and a one storey house. I opened my gate and I saw that yellow belly girl getting into her "yellow" car wearing a tight blue jeans and a smart blue tight T-shirt with her hair tied like a horse tail and in deep with her charming face. She got inside the car and zipped past in a minute.

"Daddy's princess or a Spoilt Brat?" I said to myself.

"Gosh"!! So much attitude!!!

Then I walked down for a kilometer where my cab comes to pick me up.

A month had passed and I kept on looking and looking for that yellow belly female but she was and wasn't there. I saw her a lot of times in the last month and I think she did the same .I saw her everyday our eyes almost met sometimes but she then snatched the gaze away from me and used to vanish. She was a girl, who was rude, arrogant, no mannerism because some days my mother used to stand with me but she never greeted me although ok we were not friends and we haven't seen each other at least she could greet my mom because she is elder and we are neighbours and that too sharing the same wall. She was a rich and a rude brat who has a snob about her and I knew she was not a good human being and was also heartless. She was a girl with huge arrogance and low on emotions.

One day I reached office pretty early. I was the second one to enter the office after the peon of my office because I had a lot of work to finish. I got dropped at the office by an auto-rickshaw. My work place is located in the middle of the city which is about 15 minutes away from home. I share an office with 35 other people called as colleagues in a fairly generic modern three storey office building at City Centre. It has big picture windows and on the clear days I can see the Gwalior hill and if you go to the window you can see the full view of Gwalior and see that we are surrounded by low frosted hills and with few houses on the other side of the Valley. At my work place, my staff members are polite and cooperative (that should be said) though they are not. There is a computer in every table. There are some rules for every staff member in the work place. New office furniture, bad air conditioning, and my desks or screens are visible to most of the office which is behind me. That's no good for looking at Facebook, pictures of girls, cars when I m supposed to be working. My desk is always clear and tidy. I seem to have the offices' of disposal stationaries so I have one empty can with plastic pens, rulers and erasers. Every table is very neat and clean and is loaded with papers and customers because I work in a bank, a very well-known bank of ICICI. And it's filled with customers every day. I was working on my project which was to be submitted today in the evening and I was working on it. It was 3:09 pm.

"Tringggg!!!", "Tringgggg!!!"; The desk phone beeped

"Hello!" I said.

"Varun! I want you in my cabin, now!!!" My boss said strongly.

"I will be there in a minute Sir"; I said being polite.

Wearing a white shirt and a grey pant rounding it with a black leather belt and black shoes to match with it, my hair was well set and with my beard trimmed nice, I looked decent and smart. I reached the glass cabin where my boss sits. I knocked at the glass twice. "Knock Knock..." And he ordered me to come inside.

I entered his office and there was boss sitting on his seat; a very lean man who had an angular face, thick black moustaches and protruding eyes which were covered by his big round glasses like the bottom of the coco-cola glass bottle. He was wearing a green shirt and with a knotted maroon tie, which looked totally mismatched and looked awful. His cabin was really modern with a separate air conditioner which was a bonus. He had a huge round table which was made of glass and aluminum and looked classy. A nice new black Dell PC. It's cool as nobody else can see his screen and tell that he was looking at A. rated sites!

He had a nice glass folder which was fixed on the desk with a lot of papers, an ICICI bank calendar on the wall to his right and a couple of pics of his family on the table (making him work I guess).

"Yes sir! You called me?" I said and as I stood in front of him across the table.

"Yes Varun!! Is your project ready?" He snapped without looking up from his Dell PC screen.

I checked the time on my watch and it was 3:27 pm.

"Sir, I will submit it by 7:00 pm positively!" I replied very politely.

"VARUN!!! He almost shouted. I want it in my hands by 6:00 pm anyhow!! Thank you and now you may go back to work!!!" He pulled up his bottled eyes from his screen and looked at me. And waited for me to leave.

I almost banged on his glass door but managed to control my anger and calmed down. I don't know he has some problem with me because there are things which he doesn't know about work and he forward sit the other colleagues and they end up asking me or my colleague friends and I wonder what he does behind the huge black Dell PC.

"Asshole"! I said as I reached my desk and I wanted to throw him out from those frosted hills.

I completed my work by 5:47 pm and I took the folder and went to my bosses cabin again to throw them on his ridiculous angular face but gave him before time and he saw me like he wasn't able to see me and I gave it to him on his hands.

After having a really bad day at work I took the office cab. I took the window seat of the Maruti van and was thinking of the bad day and thinking how to kill my boss (which wasn't possible). My stop came and the cab stopped. As I was getting out of the van something got hitched on to my leg and as a response I fell from the cab and I had fallen on my knees with my hands to support. I got up and saw that my right hand was bleeding and my favourite grey pant was torn from the knees. I looked for my leather bag and it was all torn and all the files, folders, calculators, pens and pencils were scattered on the floor. And I had to walk for good about a kilometer. I was collecting my things and managing to put them together because it was already dark. As I took my files and collected them and started to walk my knees hurt. With my hurt knees and bleeding hands, I was limping a bit. Just then a car with its headlights on and without any dipper; was honking like an insane creature which was definitely low in patience, because I was limping and as yes I was walking in the middle of the road slowly trying to shift to the left side of the road. As I started to walk then a car stopped just beside me. A girl with black gorgeous eyes with a charming and a graceful face who was driving the car lowered her window pane sitting by the driver window.

"Excuse me!!!Excuse me!!!" The girl shouted.

I pulled my head up and saw that it's the same girl with the yellow bellies or my neighbour or the rich rude girl. She shouted and asked "Excuse me! "Can I drop you home?"

I wondered that the girl who never looked at me and never even thought that even I existed is asking me for a lift and that too, on her own? I was confused but I was obliged to her and very thankful that now I don't have to walk a kilometer. I opened the door of her yellow Figocar and got in and sat near her she smelled awesome like a mystic rose flower which smelled awesome and that directly stroked and make me feel illusive. The stereo was full on volume and she was listening to "yellow" by Coldplay. I thought to myself —'does she has everything yellow; the songs, her car, her shoes everything! That's hilarious…' I sat inside the car and thanked her. She wore a pink dress which had white polka dots on them. Her soft face with round cheek bones, proportionally slim and sharp nose, high non-trimmed brows, and round black eyes with thick lashes, soft thin pink lips, and a rounded chin is complimented by her easy, charming smile. Though, there is a hint of a wild spark lingering behind those eye lids. She adorns jet black hair and she looks flawless. "Thank you"— I greeted her with her smile and told her it was of great help.

She gave the most wondrous SMILE with lots of innocence engraved in it, that I have ever seen in my life.

"Hi! I am Varun." I introduced myself to her while she lowered the music volume to low.

"I am your neighbour." I added!!

"I am Aisha!!!!!!" She said in a sophisticated voice and gave me a smile!:

Trust me she had the best smile in the whole universe. She has the sweetest SMILE in this whole world. She was different and I could feel it. In these six minutes till we reached home she didn't looked at me or said a word and even I find it awkward to start on with something to talk. She would find me like the other guys who flirt.

"Here you go your house has come" — she said.

"You know that I live here"— I asked being inquisitive about what she thinks of me.

"Obviously I have seen you, else I wouldn't have dropped you home"— she snapped!!

"Oh yeah!!!" — I replied and thought to myself —'SO much ATTITUDE!!!!!!!!'

"Good night Aisha, and thank you for the lift!" I said as I shut the door close.

"Good night"— she replied!

And dragged her yellow ford Figo into her garage.

Today I woke up pretty early, at around 7 am (way too early, it was because of the yellow belly girl whose name is Aisha). She made me stay awake throughout the night. Her smile was so magnificent. She had the best smile on the earth and for this smile anyone can do anything for or die for her. For that SMILE! It was a quiet morning and after a hot night. Yes, Gwalior is very hot nowadays but in the morning it was really refreshing. The sun had risen but it was mild so it was quite cool and I went out to my balcony where the chilly morning breeze greeted me. I saw the children from the neighbourhood cricket summer camp playing to become tomorrow's Sachin, Sourav, and Dravid. The sound of the boys with a background score provided by cuckoos and Indian mynas delighted me. Seeing those little boys I was lost into my own childhood when the summer vacation was real fun. I got ready for office and I was standing in the garage checking a few mails in my Blackberry phone and I could hear some giggling of a girl. Yes, it was Aisha!

She was playing with her dog (the black pup) inside her garage and I could see her from the division of our walls. It was a happy puppy ready to play with anything and to chew on everything. The flying ball would send the puppy tripping over itself in excitement and the same excitement was in Aisha's eyes!!

Her mane was glimmering down towards her shoulders where it ends, with perfectly cut tips. The uniform hair spills down between her shoulder blades in a bladed formation, the rest of it was cropping in a circular fashion towards her shoulders where the shortest strands just barely tickled the skin of her collar bone. This young woman has a soft neck and narrow shoulders that form into equally lithe arms and hands, but her mid-section shouldn't go without notice. Overall her general shape is a toned, hourglass figure defining her breast and hips which are of moderate shape, and with a wondrous SMILE on her face that was really magnificent! Yes, today she looked at me and our eyes met and she gave me a small sweet courtesy smile which took my heart and quickly stole her gaze from me.

"At least a smile! Thank god" — I said to myself.

Then I went off to office. Few days had passed and again see made me feel that I never existed 'again'. I have always seen girls dying for me whether in school, college or even office. But this girl made me feel that I never existed. Who's that girl? Who's Aisha? She's a girl who doesn't even make me feel I am there. It was after two months from the day Aisha dropped me home. I was on the terrace lighting my ultra-mild Classic cigarette and was throwing the smoke in the air and was listening to my favourite song "TUM MILE".

It was 1 am and the reflection of the moon was seen on the surface of a stream of water caused because of the rain in the evening, as clear as crystal, pure as a blanket of snow. Dark-grey clouds loomed over the moon ominously and the stream of water was perished and brought to despair and darkness once again. I saw a car around 1:45 am that stopped near my house and I thought that some friend of mine must have come to see me after getting drunk. No it wasn't my friend it was a car which was full with girls except the driver. A girl came out and the another and another came and she was.... Wait a minute I know the third girl. It's Aisha!!! Followed by Aisha another girl stepped out!

My eyes froze at Aisha. She was wearing a sophisticated brown dress which was ending a lot above her knees, her legs were like they are made of butter and looked smooth and shiny And her footwear was also of brown colour. I always had a good sense of dressing and I have never found anyone with such a lovely sense of dressing. She has an awesome and unique sense of dressing. I was trolling on the terrace and loving the weather and my cigarette of course and listening to the songs on my playlist. I could hear some giggles of some girls. Girls can giggle at the tiniest of things where a man can absolutely be very normal at the same thing. The giggles were getting louder and before I could think of anything else I saw three girls on the terrace of "Roy Mansion" which was combined just divided with a wall. I could see Ai....! Oh! No, Aisha wasn't there. I saw the three girls saw them for a few seconds and turned to the other side and checked myself quickly. I was wearing navy blue boxers and a white T-shirt with a V-neck line. The girls were humming a song but Aisha was humming a different tune. I saw Aisha as she came to the terrace humming a different tune. I was dazzled when I looked at her. Her thick, wavy, long black hair gracefully fell down to her shoulders and encircled her round-shaped face. A golden suntan usually brings out her smooth, clear complexion and high cheek bones. Her slightly arched chestnut black eyebrows highlight her emotions by moving up and down as she reacts to her world around her. Her large deep dark black eyes, remind me of a lake on a stormy day. Her sharp nose gives her the look of a little girl that makes me want to smile when she talks. And her mouth is a small mouth outlined by puffy lips that she often accentuates with glossy pink lipstick. When she smiles, which is often, her well formed and even, her white teeth brighten up her whole face. She was wearing a white Ganji and hot pink pants with little white hearts on them. And she was looking so HOT! One word for her was "WOW"! She looked hot and she looked graceful at the same time. She was unique and she was Aisha! I am sure god took a lot of time to sculpture her. She passed by me and made me feel I wasn't present there as I never existed. I was staring at Aisha and I was looking at her she has all the beauty in the whole world.

"OUCH!!!!!!" I shouted because I burnt my hand with my cigarette.

All the girls turned to me and last one who turned to me was Aisha.

"Hey"! You here?

"Yeah was having my cigarette." I replied!

"What happened? Why did you shout?" She asked and started to walk towards me. With her glamorous face.

"Actually I burnt my hand with the cigarette." I replied!

"You Ok? Or you need some ice?" Aisha showed care as she enquired,

"No! No! I am really Ok! Thank you Aisha!"

A girl came and stood near Aisha and she introduced me to her four friends. She pointed out to each girl and said she's Sujata, Mandakini, Aparajita and Swati. I said a "HI" to all as a courtesy but

I wasn't very keen to know. And Aisha told her friends "Girls he is...ummmm"!!

"Excuse me! Sorry! Your name?" asked Aisha showing a questioning gesture and asked my name.

"Hello! I am Varun! :"

Sujata and Mandakini said "Hi" followed by Aparajita and Swati. But I was a little ashamed because I was in my boxers with so many girls in front of me and I was in my Bloody boxers. Why is always luck so hard on me I wondered! I thought of leaving and waved good-bye as they were busy on their own but inside my heart I wanted to stay with Aisha. This was happening to me for the first time that I am being attracted to a girl. Every time it has been that girls get attracted to me but AISHA she was different. I waved and reached my terrace door, suddenly a feminine voice with immense sweetness like it was warm and flowing like hot chocolate, and everyone seemed to relax when she had something to say.

"Hey Varun"! — Somebody called! It was Aisha!

My heart skipped a beat and I was overwhelmed and excited that she called my name. She wants me with her. What will she say? Does she like me too? Like? Do I Like her? Am I falling for her? Am I? How can this be possible? I never fell for anyone. All these things were going inside my head and suddenly I trembled when Aisha called out for me again.

"Varun! Varun!!" Aisha called,

"Yes, sorry I was a little lost. Yes tell me" — I replied,

"Varun if you don't mind can I get a cigarette"— Aisha said.

"Oh yeah, Sure". I took out my Classic ultra-mild's cigarette packet from the right pocket of my boxers which was grey in colour and took the box and she was near the division of our walls where any of us could like jump the wall and be together but I was beneath the walls and so was she. I took the box and gave it to Aisha. Though I don't like girls having cigarette, I don't have a problem with them having but I don't like it and that's my vision. Some boys find it as a turn on when they see girls having cigarette. Aisha took a cigarette from the box and said "Thank you Varun"!

"You can take one more". I said and smiled as I passed the pack.

"No! No!! My friends want to have. I don't smoke actually I hate smoking and cannot take the smoke. So thank you Varun, one is enough." She replied.

And I was happy with the fact that Aisha doesn't smoke. I don't know why but I was Happy.

They all thanked me for the cigarette and I started walking (not towards Aisha, Walk towards the terrace door.) I alarmed myself.

"Varun!!!" A voice came which was sounding general, it did not make too much movement. I thought and I was pretty sure that Aisha wants me to accompany them. But I turned back and saw one of her friends called me. It was Swati I guess. They all were sitting on the bean bags in a circle and had a small round baby pool and they were sitting around it that had lights on. And I could see some alcohol bottles there.

"Hay ohayo Varun! Can I borrow your lighter for a second?" Swati or Sujata I guess (I forgot the names) left the bean bag and came up to the boundary and I did the same. She took the lighter, she was around 5'7" in height and had a nice built not fat but was a healthy and fit looking girl. She lighted up her cigarette and threw a mist and said "wow this is what I call chilling"!

"Thanks, thanks Varun" — Swati or Sujata replied— I think she has a habit of repeating words.

"My pleasure". I sounded Gentle.

And I was thinking Aisha wants me to accompany them. Such a big fool I am. And I was thinking Aisha will call me to accompany her and to sit with them at two am in the morning. I am such a bloody idiot!!!! I came downstairs and went straight into my room and directly stood in front of the mirror to check myself. Did I look awful?

Rubbing my chin and closely noticing. Hmmmm …hair … with a little spikes and short hair made me look sexy and smart at the same time, light beard and my fair face with a dimple on my left cheek is the best I have, and girls die for my dimples. I am five feet and ten inches tall not bad at all and girls like tall boys or men. Hmmm… my physique is not that built up like any Hollywood or Bollywood star but I have a lean body with broad shoulders and arms. The only thing which will bring my image down are my "Blue boxers" 9

Oh god….! Why did I……?

"Aaaahhhhhhhhhhhhh…".A loud scream from outside came and I was trying to locate the source from where the voice was coming.'

Aaaahhhhhhh…Ahhhhhhhhh…". It came again. And it was coming from the terrace and I knew it was the girls. I climbed up to the stairs as fast as I could like the Metro trains on its tracks to reach the terrace. Sometimes I think girls can giggle at the tiniest of things and shout on their top of their voices at things when they are the minutest. When I reached the terrace what I saw was AISHA (My Aisha) was holding the pup the same pup which she picked up from the road the day I saw Aisha for the very first time. The other girls were shouting because they thought that they have seen a monster. (Are you afraid of dogs? Don't be they are the best things which has been gifted to humans. Be with them and you will see happiness all around you when they are around you.)

Aisha was holding the black little pup in her hands and very close to her neck like she was carrying a human baby and she was at one end of the terrace and the three girls were at one side of the terrace as they were frightened and one was talking on her phone sitting on her bean bags beside the pool.

"What happened"? I asked out of anxiety.

"Oh! They are afraid of the twenty-five days old German shepherd". — looking at the girls she answered in her sweet voice plus loads of attitude immersed in her voice.

The pup was black in colour and had some golden fur on the middle of his and had small paws and a tiny thin tail that was hanging around Aisha's neck which was making me jealous I wish I was in place of the dog.

"They were shouting because of this?" — I was a little shocked as I said.

"Ha Ha Ha!!! Yeah" — Aisha laughed.

And her smile, her laugh was something that looked beautiful on her and could warm the coldest of hearts. A free and infectious gift that radiates from the mouth as muscles in the cheeks tighten to show enjoyment in the simple pleasure of the moment, bringing a sparkle of vigour to empty eyes. If even for an instant, a smile of her gave me an uplifting feeling and show of charm which was given to me from Aisha. She was beautiful and her smile her laugh was the best think I have ever seen in my whole life.

"I was so terrified that what has happened to you guys"— I replied.

"He he he!!" Aisha giggle and she looked like an angel. Her smile was wow.

"Aisha what's your dog's name?" I asked thinking she will get happy.

"Excuse me Varun! His name is Ronaldo"— she said sounding very stern and angry.

'Don't call him a dog". She added and warned me as well.

"Oops so sorry." (And I was killing myself inside for calling the dog as a dog) — I apologised.

Ronaldo! The man with the golden boot I have always seen him on television and I was seeing Ronaldo in real. God this was Hilarious. I am sure Ronaldo the name was given by Aisha, it was just like her. Unique.

She kept Ronaldo on the slab of the two walls of our houses which were joined and Ronaldo was walking over it and Aisha adored her. One of her friend was still on the couch talking on the phone the other was on the opposite side of the terrace and was looking at the stars and the third one was with Aisha and was near her (the one who took the lighter Swati or Sujata) and the fourth girl wasn't visible I think she had gone downstairs.

"Can I hold him" — I asked Aisha (Buttering)

I never liked dogs not that I hated them but I wasn't like Aisha. She kisses the dog (sorry Ronaldo). I should put this in practice. She kisses it on its nose on the paws on the ears on the head. Yep, she was very different from others. She was a different flower in the garden. She was Aisha.

"Oh yes! Why not!" With full of excitement in her voice and eyes glittering and she gave me the sweetest of her smiles. Her smile sweetened the very air in my lungs.

Her tone was totally different when I asked for Ronaldo. She is only the ONE on this earth.

I took RONALDO in my hands. They are always little and gooey with this awkward puppy walk that is somewhat uncoordinated and can lead to clumsiness but luckily this didn't happen. His fur was softest and fluffiest and it had bigger amounts of puppy fat around their necks. They always have the biggest watery eyes and little sweet and the gentle noses.

I was playing with Ronaldo and Aisha and three of her friends took their glasses and had their drink. I guess it was alcohol but the fourth one wasn't visible. But Aisha's eyes were on me to check if I was good to the pup or not. I played with Ronaldo for a while (though I never wanted to) but just to be with Aisha I was with the Lucky German Shepherd. It was with me for some minutes but after that he started avoiding me and made a 'Koooon..... kooooon' noise from which Aisha understood that the lucky black pup wants to be with Aisha. Obviously, anyone would die to be with a girl like her. That's not its fault at all.

I wish I was Ronaldo! — I said to myself.

It was very late I checked my Blackberry phone for the time and it was 3:18 am and it was enough of playing with Ronaldo, I was about to start the conversation with her as I was never afraid of talking to any girl in my life but this time I was afraid and this was killing me inside. And I couldn't understand the reason. After many attempts of starting the conversation, When I uttered Ai.........

Aauuuu….. Aisha made a irritably look.

The mosquitoes were biting her. Swati or Sujata was also standing with her but she didn't complain. I don't blame the mosquitoes even. She so sweet her blood must be having a unique taste as well. She called her friends and said "let's go downstairs (neeche chalte hai)".

"Han let's go, I am hungry"— the bean bag girl said.

"Me too"— Aisha said.

They started to move and I said "GOOD NIGHT" like a slave.

Her fiends wished me good night and Aisha wished me at the last. A strong windy breeze blew and this made her hair fly which came on her face and she gently removed it and looked the most amazing girl I have ever seen. Her coquetry, her sophisticated behaviour, and her moves her hand the way she walks it is so graceful. I was totally drowned in her. I was thinking all this and then I realised I was the only one standing on the terrace they all had gone and I was standing like a fool and a stupid lunatic.

And that reminds me of how lunatic I am. I have to prepare a presentation for my bank tomorrow and it was 4:17 am and I have to reach office by 10 am sharp and my presentation will take place at 12 noon. I was so screwed.

"Oh Bloody shit! Crap Crap!!! I am dead!!!"

My alarm clock buzzed but I snooze it and sleep back to my bed.

My alarm buzzed and checked the time it was six am and I jumped from the bed as I was supposed to get up by 5 a.m. Today I will be fired I cannot do the whole thing in this short time. I just slept for an hour last night. I was in a hurry I just peeped into Aisha's garage but couldn't see her but her yellow Figo was there in her garage. I couldn't wait for her because I was almost screwed and I will be totally screwed if I waste one minute here. I entered office the same office as I described to you earlier. I was in a hurry and totally stressed. I reached my table. I was working on my presentation when…

"Hello Varun! Good morning dear!" — Ria said (she is one of my colleagues with whom I went on a date she is tall and has a normal slim figure but she's not my type and I don't like her but she's always hitting on me).

"Ria don't irritate. I have a lot of work to do"— I snapped.

"Varun! You don't even talk to me these days" — Ria said in her flirtatious tone.

"Ria…disappear right now" — I almost shouted.

She left my table and gave me a nasty look.

It was 11:57 am and I was done with my presentation but had not prepared for it.

It was 12 noon and I was done and was waiting for the presentation which was to take place in the conference hall. I was preparing and was waiting for everyone to come. I was nervous as my boss, he would not leave any point to assault me in any kind. If he found me with any error or any unanswered question he will put down my image in front of all. So, I wanted to make it the best and impress my bosses boss so that I can get promoted and kick my bosses ass.

The presentation started at 12:45 pm which was pretty good for me some times luck showers on me. My bosses boss took the head seat of the conference table. My boss with his Coco-Cola bottom glasses took the next one in the vertical line and nine more of us joined in including Ria and I took the bottom seat opposite to my Super boss. I wore a clean white shirt with a grey pant to go with it and a perfect decent leather belt and shoes polished with the leather shine which I did it in a minute. The presentation started and I was confident. I was put up with some silly and logical questions from my cylindrical boss and the others respectively and I put them in their shoes and answered it pretty well I suppose. The presentation ended on a good note and my Super boss was very happy with me.

"You will go on a long run"— He shook hands with me and went. My boss looked at me like he will inhale and kill me. I gave him a stern look and went off to my desk.

"You were really good" — Ria said.

"Thank you Ria!" — I replied.

"Let's go out somewhere"— She said.

"No Ria, I don't want to. Thank you for your invitation but I cannot go." I replied.

It has never been ever in my life that I have denied somebody for a date or going out with a girl in the evening. Something was changing inside me or it was the work stress.

She went off without saying a word.

After a tiring day as well the night; I was really tired but very happy because the presentation turned out be quite well. And I was thinking I was screwed. Thank God!!!

I was working on my desk and it was 3:24 pm and I was actually drooling on my desk as I had slept only for an hour. I dreamt for a minute I guess. But I couldn't make out whether I was dreaming or was it reality. I saw Aisha. And shook my head again to remove the illusion and get back to reality. Why was I so into her? Why am I dreaming of her in the day? What is wrong with me? I shook my head and looked at the same way. But I saw her again. I shook again and ....

OH GOD!! OH MY MY!!!! IT IS "AISHA"!!!!!!!!!!

It is Really Aisha????

She was wearing a tight fitted jean which was black in colour. And a top which was had blue as a base and a little transparent at the top and followed by cream and orange broad stripes and she was looking like a model. She was looking sexy. She looked beautiful. She looked graceful and she looked truly beautiful. And her hair was straight and black which ended near her waist.

YES! She was there in front of my eyes. Oh yes!

She was talking to an executive and after a while she was on the phone and walking towards another executive. After a short delay I realised she was walking towards me. She was walking towards me???? God!!!!!! I was incited. My heart filled with excitement and I quickly checked myself by turning off my computer screen which was on my desk after the PC turned out to be black I checked and I was looking like a drunkard. My eyes had swollen and my hair was good but wasn't perfect and I wasn't in my best. Last night she saw me in boxers and today like a drunkard. Why is she with me when I am at my worst? And I wasn't dressed properly yes I said I was dressed well before but not according to Aisha and her class. I was checking out myself and........

"Excuse me"...! A voice said which was sweet and velvety, but was embraced with a lot of confidence.

I put my head up and it was yeah (you are right) it was Aisha.......

And then her head lifted from the papers she had in her hand, and her gaze met mine.

Her face was perfect in its balance of curves and lines: a beautifully arched nose, high cheekbones, rich lips curved into a smile.

A thick tumble of auburn hair fell slightly past her shoulders.

Her limbs were long and graceful, calling to mind a willow bending elegantly in the breeze.

But it was her eyes that truly caught me: black with bean, like the sunlight shining through summer leaves.

For a moment I felt the urge to remove my hat like.

I was in the presence of the queen herself.

I cleared my throat and managed to say "Yes"!!

"Oh Hi! Hi Aisha" — I said. "How are you"? I added. (Like I was born in a formality class)

"Hey!!!!Varun right?" With exclamation and excitement in her voice.

"So you work here?" She added, before I could say anything else.

"You guessed it right Madame. Please sit" — I said and pointed out to the seat in front of me.

"So how can I help you Aisha Ma'am? " I quoted.

"Actually, Mr. Banker!!! Your bank is really troubling me a lot, so now I am thinking of changing my bank. I want to take out my currency and I will shift it to the other bank. Your bank has lot of tantrums.

"I apologise for all the bothering which happened to you"— can you please tell me your problem Ma'am!

"You can call me Aisha!" — She replied. Your bank is not delivering my credit card and my check book. I have been checking but I didn't receive and it has been a month almost.

"Listen Mr. Manager". It is my company account and a current account as well so if you people will trouble me like this it would be difficult for me to continue with this bank — She snapped angrily.

"I am sorry Miss Aisha"— I apologised.

"I will just check it out and tell you where is it placed"— I rejoined.

"The credit card is not that important but I want my check book as soon as possible and that too within two days else I cannot continue business with your bank"— she snapped back.

She speaks to hard and deep and she talks mature. I haven't come across a girl who is intelligent as well way too beautiful. I have always across pretty girls but dumb and always conquer boys and dates. She was different. She was talking business like any intellectual personality at her early twenties. I was enthralled by her talking skills and her mental level. Girl with beauty and brains.

I was also annoyed with my bank because it was troubling my Aisha. Without warning I wanted to fire all and blast all the senior people of my back. And then I realised and made myself calm and said to myself.

"Buddy you work here" Don't kick your job and act like a prey of shark. And I was back to normal else because of Aisha I would have jump into the water with sharks.

"Give me two minutes Ma'am. I will just check it out". I entered her bank account number and yes she was a priority member and I was going through her account and could see a whole lot of money and that made me a little sad inside. I couldn't understand the reason. I was sad because a rich girl like her will not even be my friend. She is not in my reach she is out of my reach and I fell poignant. I offered her some water to drink but she didn't even look at it and said Thank you and denied to have it. Brashness with a snob attitude in her persona.

"Mr. Mall" (Mall is my surname she said it because my name board was on my table). I think she has a habit of calling people from different names. This was the third different name in the last half an hour.

"When will I get my cheque book? If you can tell me the exact date?" — Aisha enquired.

"You will be happy to know that your cheque book is here"— I smiled as I answered.

"Oh that's nice" — her anger changed into a smirk. "Can you give it to me now? She queried.

I could have given the cheque book then and there. But I wanted to spend some time with Aisha so I said you have to wait for some time because it is in the store and to locate it will need some time. (It was just I could spend some time with Aisha) but I was acting different this time. I never wanted to be with any girl and following and getting attracted wasn't me at all. I was acting insane.

"How much time will it take?" Asked Aisha.

"Just a few minutes may be 15 minutes from now"— as I called the store manager to asked her to locate it and tell him "through phone".

"Are you in a rush?" — I added. (I enquired as if I was anxious whether she was going on a date or what).

"Yep Varun! I am in a rush and I have to reach factory ASAP."

"Factory???" I relied with a shocked gaze.

"You work in a factory?" I added — I asked out of my inquisitiveness.

"He he !!" She giggled. Her smile is the best thing to a man and anyone can fall for her smile ranging from any age. Her smile was chocolate, memorising with each syllable.

"Not really" — she replied.

What does that mean now? I hate girls when they always make thriller talks.

"That means what?" — I queried.

Actually the company account is my own company and that's a private limited company. Actually that's my dad's factory but yes we both are the owners and looking after it.

"WOW"!!!!!! That's amasing that's incredible. So, I was talking to a young lady who is an entrepreneur. That's superb. I feel honoured to talk to you"— I was dazed as I replied.

"TRINNNNNNNNNNNNNNN"……… Her phone rang. Pink coloured Swarovski back cover (thank god it wasn't yellow this time). OMG! She was using an I-phone to be more précise. No doubt she was a spoiled brat or may be a successful entrepreneur. Her eyebrows narrowed and she was disgusted when she asked something she was scolding someone that I understood from her tone and her words but she was scolding at a really low pitch. (Man how does she do that?) And all this while I was just gazing at her like a little puppy and looking at her charming and gorgeous face.

"Varun"!" she called out my name as she disconnected the phone.

"Varun, can you do me a favour ?" She demanded.

"Yes tell me what is it?" — I murmured.

"Can you please locate the cheque book and keep it with you. So tomorrow on my way to work I will pick up the cheque book and rush." — She said.

"I think you are forgetting" — I sounded witty.

"What?" — She gazed.

"You are forgetting that because I am your neighbour and I can give you the cheque book as well as the credit card today at your place at around 8:00 pm sharp Ma'am." — I replied smartly.

"Can you do that for me? That would be a BIG help for me" — She answered. Her hair came in front of her face as the air conditioner panes moved towards her and she was managing them to settle in the same way and when she was doing it trust me she looked flawless, she looked way too beautiful and charming.

"Yes! Yes!! Why not? I will be obliged Madame"— I gave her a smirk.

She left the seat and started to walk towards the bank main gate and I followed her to see her off and shook hands with her (which was firm and strong, very less people have this type of handshakes) I was impressed. She waved good-by and said "Thank you!!"

I was walking through the office floor and Ria eyed me because I never gave so much importance to anyone. As she was so pretty and sexy she would have been jealous for sure and I behaved as if she wasn't in front of my eyes. I was blushing a bit because I have received Aisha's smile and this was like a present which was tied in ribbons and was smelling awesome. I was at my uttermost excitement because tonight I was going to meet Aisha at her place (It seemed like a date to me) but I wasn't going on a date with her 9 pm. But I was happy!!!! As I was rejoicing and enjoying my excitement and elation my phone rang "TrinTrinTrin"!!!!

"Golu calling"!!!!

Ok Golu is my friend who used to take me to Angela the coffee shop. He was my first friend in Gwalior and now my best friend. He's always there for me when I am in need. He's there to kick my ass whenever I made a mistake. He was there in all my good and bad times. He was there when I was sick he was there when I was a drunken beast. He was there when I used to go on dates and at my place I was with Golu. He's my best friend. He's everything he's a person to fight and then get back together like nothing ever happened.

Friendship is for a lifetime,

With kicks and love at times,

I was with a friend whom I was guessing,

Golu is a friend whom I got as a blessing.

Now-a-days he is in Bangalore, doing a job in an IT company after completing his engineering in Information Technology from Amity University.

So, Golu is my friend. So, whenever he's pissed happy or drunk. He calls me for sure because I do the same when I am jerk and he listens to me very patiently and I do the same I guess not like him but yes to a point. But it was 3:17 pm and it wasn't a weekend and he's not drunk why he is calling me now. I wish everything is fine with him because we don't call each other on a regular basis but we are the best friends when we talk it feels that we met yesterday.

Finding friends with the same mental disorder as you.... PRICELESS"!!!!!!

"You *kuttakamina*", how much time you need to receive a phone call and that too from me?" — Golu shouted on top of his voice with anger.

"What is keeping you so busy that you cannot reply to my messages? And you need so much time to receive my call! You Moron!" — He blasted before I could say anything.

"How are you buddy"? — I replied.

"I am budding"— he teased. You remember now "how is your buddy? Asshole"— He teased and snapped.

"Ha hahahaha" — I replied. I was laughing out real loud.

"Listen I will be coming to Gwalior next weekend. As my house will be locked because my parents are going out of town."— He said.

"Then why you are coming?" — I queried.

"You idiot it is Richa's birthday the coming weekend. (Richa is his girlfriend). So I will be staying with you at your place" — He demanded.

"Are you taking permission for me for staying at my place"? — I sounded humorous.

"No you fucker, I am informing you and demanding you to stay there when I come. So I was just informing you" — He demanded.

"Ha ha !Aye Aye Sir. Which date are you coming and by which train" — I asked.

"I will message you the details by tonight Ok" — he replied calmly.

"Mr. Varun Mall, You fucker by the way why are you sounding so happy? May I know the reason?" — he enquired.

"Am I? Really? Seriously? No no! Just like that. "— I protested.

"Who's the girl this time man"? — He said drolly.

I was surprised as if he was sitting just next to me and he could see all the things which happened in the last half an hour. Oh god, it's like he can sense my nerves. My heart was beating fast and I could feel it.

And what time and what art,

Could twist the sinews of my heart

And when my heart began to beat

And what dread skin and what dread soul.

I bowed my head on the table and quickly reformed and I wondered how on earth he knew about it.

"It is Aisha" — I replied tenderly.

He was laughing at the other end yes LOUD.

"I am coming on 26th April. Did you take her number?" — He sounded stirring.

"No yaar I just met her and she's so arrogant" — I replied woefully.

"You come and then we will talk about that female who is playing with my brains" — I added quickly.

"Ok cool. See you soon then"— He replied and he disconnected the phone.

I went back to work and checked Aisha's account as her page was still on my screen. I was looking at her accounts and then I was checking her debits and credits and as I was escaping her page. I found something. It was Aisha's phone number 9990005999. When I saw her number I actually felt like dancing. I felt to dance on my work table and then on the work floor followed by the chair. Then I thought I shouldn't dance and quietly sit down else people will throw shoes on me and it made me realise I am in office. I was actually acting mad. I tossed my head and got back to basic and quickly saved her number in my blackberry phone and I saved it in capitals "AISHA". The top most name in my contact list. After locating and taking the credit card and check book in my drawer I got back to work but I was tired and feeling assaulted because it was a very tiring day in addition I skipped my sleep and that too for a girl whom I don't know but she was special and she was beautiful. I was working but down the line I was truly excited about the evening meeting with her. I had butterflies in my stomach this was the first time that thinking of meeting a girl is giving me butterflies. I looked at my watch it was 5:32 pm and I thought to leave by 7:00 pm sharp and swiftly calculated to reach Aisha. I had 5 cups of coffee and as I became conscious that I wasn't going for an interview or not to propose to my girl friend, I was going to meet my client who was my neighbor and she was Aisha to just handover the cheque book and the credit card to her. That's it. I checked out the clock of our bank it struck 6:29 pm and I started to wind up my work. And I saw the coco-cola bottled eyed man walking towards me (Yes, I am talking about my boss.)

He came and I stood up and wished him. He nodded and replied.

Coco-cola bottled man (My boss) said to me "you are doing a good job. Great job done."— he said with gratitude.

"Thank you sir"— I replied sincerely.

"Regarding your presentation, we have a brief meeting in five minutes. Come to my cabin now."— My boss ordered and walked off to his cabin.

The coco-cola bottled man whose self-interest always comes first, his chief drive is to constantly curry favour with senior managers at higher levels in the organisation (without sharing credit with his staff employees). The habitually secretive man withholds information as a way to control people, which is endangering my trust and originating anger towards him. The information soaked into my mind before my heart. I clenched my fists so hard, nails digging into my palms. Fury raced through my body, heating me to my very core and igniting a flame so hot within my heart that I almost screamed in agony and anger. Why couldn't he tell me before? A meeting in five minutes that is so ridiculous. If I was a superman or a spiderman I would have slapped my boss on his face pretty hard and grab him down on the floor flat and kick his ass and made him fall as a summer sault. (But then I said to myself I am not a superhero, I am a normal being). And nodded my head like a slave. I wish I could do what I just thought. I checked my watch it was 6:45 pm and I so wanted to bunk the meeting but I couldn't because I was not the boss and the boss is always right. I wanted to be with her I wanted her in front of my eyes.

The meeting ended and it was 7:12 pm I rushed for home immediately. I was never in a hurry for anything whether it is play or work, but today every second was beating my nerves. Sometimes it was so intense that I skipped my breath and for an instance I was suffocating. I actually never cared for anyone in my whole life I have been to hundreds of dates but haven't felt like this before. I felt something is different. It was a different feeling altogether I was different. Why am I feeling different? Is it because of the beautiful chick? Was I falling for that person? I had huge expectations about my feelings because I was the intense feeling for the first time. Is it because of Aisha? But I wonder if she will like me? Will she love me? Or she loves somebody else? Loves? IS SHE SINGLE? My heart was beating faster just thinking about that person. My heart lurches for fear that will she even like me. My stomach ties itself in knots when I am apart and I long to see her again. I want to hold her hand day and night. I want to kiss her lips and never want to stop.

Oh my Aisha is like the red rose,

That's freshly sprung in June

Oh my love is the sweet melody,

That sweetly plays its tune.

But was she single or committed or even engaged? I was scared of thinking all this. I want her in my life I just want her I am in love with Aisha. I Love her..........

But I was scared! Scared? Wriggling worms crawled up and down my spine and creating a sickening sensation difficult to control. With the soft and sweet feeling of love there are negative feelings like fear of rejection, loosing are dearly attached. It is the duality of love. Small beads of perspiration formed on my upper lip and waves of heat and cold swept over me, like having fever fighting for control of my body. I couldn't think of anything but just the rejection from My Love. My happiness and excitement changed into dismay. I started to think all those stuffs which never came to my thoughts.

She was charming like a princess

And independent like a fowl,

She has pleasant gestures

This made her One of all.

I was driving home today. And I missed my way home and this was all because of her. It was like I was turning into soup and my inner body was like having fireworks go off inside you.

I was in love! I never thought of being in love and that too like an arrogant and a snob girl like her but obviously beautiful at its peak. I had an equal mixture of pure ecstasy and pure pain. I was feeling pathetic and helpless.....but in a lovely way!

I had reached home. And it was 7:39 pm though I was a little late and I pushed my car into my garage and locked up the door and went inside. I didn't even peeped inside Aisha's house as I was sad.

Oh my Love, are you in the sky solo,

Or beneath the stars with the sparkles flow,

The heart out of the bosom,

Will never make you fall in vain.

I went into my room directly didn't even greet dad who was watching television in the drawing room. I kept my bag (actually threw my bag on my bed) because this was a feeling I never came across this was painful and was feeling hollow. And I walked straight into the washroom and had a shower and I was feeling much better like the thoughts have cooled down. I wore a red and blacked striped polo t-shirt of Tommy Hilfiger (yep inspired by her stripes in the morning). And I was looking pretty good. I came out and sat in the living room beside dad on a different couch.

Ma eyed me and asked — "What happened to you? And where are you going?"

"Nothing has happened what will happen" — I snapped and looking at the television without looking at her.

She gave a bowl of Maggie and I grabbed it without making any noise. I slurped it away. My mom again asked me are you Ok?

"Mom nothing just I am tired and now I have to go to a clients house have some work" — I replied rigidly.

"I don't understand when you are tired why don't you complete your work in you workplace only?" — she argued.

"My client stays in the same colony. That's why I took the work" — I argued too.

"Anything else you want to know" — I added (irritably),

"Ok! In the same locality itself. What's your customer's name? May be I know him."— Ma replied.

"She! Not he." — I said as I placed the empty bowl on the centre table of the living room.

"She?????" — She got a shock (she reacted in a way that I am a single girl who is pregnant)

"Aisha Roy. Address- B-404 Govindpuri, Gwalior." — I read it from my papers which I had in my hand.

"Aisha!!!!!! That pretty chick" she almost jumped from the couch and my dad was watching us both and didn't utter a word. She reacted like she's my girlfriend not my client.

"That pretty chick but she's more of arrogant. She never greets anyone even when I pass by or anybody else she doesn't give a damn. She's a total snob. A spoiled brat and the only daughter of her parents. They are rich that I agree but that doesn't mean you will pass by that no one near you even exists. But her mother is a nice woman. Do you know she has different car for herself"— she replied and bitched about Aisha. (Inside I was feeling angry because she was mine and I cannot listen to any bad remarks when it comes to Aisha).

"You don't have to stress son. I will give it to her mother" — She said gently.

"Ma! It's not a neighbour thing. It is business. Please!" — I almost shouted.

I collected my diary her cheque book and credit card and checked whether I have taken everything and was ready to leave. I banged the door after me. I checked my hair on the pane of the car and it was pretty cool. I peeped into her garage and the yellow Figo was still there (I don't know what makes her buy a yellow car). Ok I forgot she's a limited edition and I smiled on my own. I stood in front of the main gate of the ROY mansion. This had a huge brown wooden gate. Through which nothing was visible. The name plate outside says ROY'S which was on wooden and the name was engraved in an artistic manner not like the usual ones. I pressed the bell. I could hear some quirkiness from inside the house. And the main gate was opened by a watch man who was very good built and had a Charlie Chaplin type moustache which was hilarious. A strong, tall and a dark man with such a tiry moustache. I entered and I saw a huge garden on the left which had beautiful grass with all types of flowers and the garage was huge where three different cars were resting. A lady in her middle age opened the door from her living room her skin is whitish color. Her lips are large and pink, and her eyes are very big and brown. Her hair is short and wavy which reaches her shoulders. It is a rich black color, with strands of grey, which have appeared over the past few years. She has a smile on her face that shows her wisdom and age. She was in her early 40's wrapping a *sari* around her wiry body.

"Yes"? She queried in a polite tone.

"Aunty! I am Varun from Axis bank! I ....

"Oh yeah yeah! Come in" — she welcomed me with a smile on her face.

"Aisha told me you will be coming tonight. Come have a seat"— She pointed me to the couch of the living room.

"Thank you" — I sat and wished her.

She took the couch in front of me and said "if I am not wrong, you are Nandita's son right"?

"Yes aunty" — I replied (Nandita is my mother's name).

The house was lavish. The bricks are red on one of the walls, and there is always a light shining in at least one of the windows.

The house has a scent of pine, and the living room is painted a dazzling light blue. A sofa and matching chair are both dressed in cozy cream-coloured slip-covers. Wooden, the floor stretches all across the room with no carpet to hide it. A huge LED sits on a set by the wall. On the centre table sits a little pot of red roses and yellow lily's and exclusive candles of the matching colours of the flowers. There is a set of mahogany chairs gathered around the short round glass table. Another pot of roses is sitting in the middle of this table. But these roses are white. It is like the playing area like to play chess or cards or to just sit and gossip.

When I first looked at this house, there was a baby grand piano sitting in the living room and that was the first thing I looked at. I always wanted one of those old antebellum houses with the big wrap around porches, all hardwood floors and atleast one fireplace (it was exactly one of those kind). The house was fully furnished with inimitable antiques all over.

"Beta! What will you have?" — She asked with erudite.

"Thank you aunty! But nothing". Is Aisha home? — I asked (because I couldn't see her)

"No *beta* she's not home"— she answered normally.

Then what the hell I am doing here. She is never at home. This time I was very angry with Aisha. I am here for her work. — I said to myself.

"Ok aunty then I must leave" — I replied holding my anger in control.

"No! No! Wait dear — she said in the motherly tone. "She will be back in a while. She asked me to make you wait till she arrives." — Aisha's mother added.

Am I a stupid ass or a train on platform who's waiting the passengers to load on the train? But I cannot even see my passenger. Where the hell is she?

"Varun! She will be back in a few minutes. She has gone out for some work" — she said.

The servant came wearing a normal blue trouser and a white t-shirt with a glass of water where the glass was stylish and tray I think it was of silver. The water also tasted different. I took the glass of water and said thank you to the servant and he went. I couldn't locate Aisha's dad. I think he wasn't home.

"How is your mother *beta*" — she asked (so that obviously I don't get bored).

"She is fine aunty"— I replied.

"I have to meet her. It has been a while I haven't seen her" — she said.

"I told this girl not to go out when someone is coming to your place at the given time and when the work is yours. Somebody is coming just for you for your work so you should be thankful and not make him wait. But she doesn't listen"— Aisha's mother added.

"It is Aisha. Aisha................................." — her mother said calling out to her.

"What? What are you saying about me" Suddenly this girl came and blasted on her mother.

"Mum! What are you saying about me to him"? — Aisha almost shouted.

"Nothing dear. I was just asking him to wait till you come"— her mom protested.

"Ok! Whatever" — Aisha replied.

As soon as she walked into the room, they were all silenced, awed by her mysterious beauty. As she carried herself, pale and slender, gracefully and elegantly towards one of the men in the room (that's me), I noticed something. She seemed like a queen, high and regal, with a strange air of mystery about her. And her beauty couldn't help but add mystery to her. She had dark, dark wavy hair, with these strikingly round black round eyes, pink slim lips. She walked and sat on the couch which was just near me. She threw the car keys on the centre table near the exclusive candles and beautiful flowers. She wore a fancy royal blue top which was till her thighs and adorning with a light grey legging and she looked prettier.

"Hey Varun, thank you for coming" — Aisha said sweetly.

Loud thumping seemed to drown out all other sounds as my heart pounded against my ribs and my lungs struggled to intake sufficient air. Dizziness spells threatened to drop me to my knees and I felt my stomach contract and the sphincter muscle starts to relax, a symptom of fight or flee, creating an even greater fear of messing myself. (Because Aisha was sitting in front of me and I was deadly in love with her). No one couldn't even think for once instance she was so angry and just in a moment she was sweet as honey. She was the sweetest and the glorious person on earth. Her mom stood up and said — "I shall send something to eat. You both sit and chat." — She said and went.

I just smile as she went but I must say she is the coolest mom (mom of a girl). Because, she is allowing her daughter to talk to a guy alone who is not a friend to him at 8:45 pm.

"Aisha here is your cheque book and your credit card" — I sounded smart and handed over the cheque book to her and asked to sign on the papers of receipt. She has an urbane signature. She opened the credit card and saw like it was a magic card for her.

"Thank you so much Varun! It was really nice of you. Thank you". Her eyes sparkled with kohl above her eyes which made her look magnificent. — She said in an innocent voice.

"Ok, then Aisha I must leave"! (I never wanted to leave her because I have already fallen for her yes I was in insanely in love with her which I realised today and she is mine and I cannot afford to lose her. She will be mine one day. She is the girl I want to get married to).

"Why"????? — She enquired annoyingly.

"No no you are not going anywhere. Sit, mum is sending something to eat." — She ordered.

She was the sweetest and the most innocent girl I have ever come across and such a beautiful girl. I directly wanted to say Aisha I am in love with you. Or ask Aisha. Are you single?

"Sit sit" — She said as if she knows me from ages and I am her best friend. She was sooo friendly.

"You are from Gwalior itself?" — She asked.

"Why I don't look like the Gwalior people?" — I smirked and replied wittily.

"NO!!"— She smiled. Not at all that's why I asked you Varun. Ha ha ha!!! — She laughed.

"No I am here for the last three years only. I have done my schooling from Calcutta and then we shifted to Bombay and came to Delhi where I did my college and now in Gwalior. As my dad has a transferrable job". — I said.

"CALCUTTA???" She exclaimed

"Are you a bong"??? She asked with big dazed eyes.

"No, No I am not a bong. Just because of my dad as he has a transferrable job."

"Ohhh !! I thought so." — She replied.

"And where in Delhi you used to stay Varun?" She asked. "Actually I was studying in Delhi for my graduation thought not in Delhi my college was in Noida and I used to stay in Noida itself."— She added.

"Oh!! Even I used to stay in Noida. — That's nice."

The same servant came with a full huge exclusive tray which looked like it was pure silver and placed it on the centre table of the living room and went. They contained wafers, dry fruits, some fried nuggets and choco-chip cookies and a black colour soft drink which was in exclusive cocktail glasses and the other were served with erudite crockery's which made the snack look delicious. The smell of the nuggets was mouth-watering and I wanted to grab them but Aisha was there and I had to behave sophisticatedly just like her. Oh god she is a beauty.

"Varun ! Please take it. Help yourself please." — She said and sounded friendly. And took one of the unique glasses where the cold drink was served. She took it from her right hand and indicated me to take the other glass (I thought she will hand over the glass to me just as a gesture). But No!

She took the glass and went back to her couch and relaxed.

"You can take the Glass Varun. You don't have to feel shy at all and I cannot do the formality thing. So please take these and relax." — She said.

She pointed at the nuggets and said "taste the chicken nuggets. They are really yum. Obviously, if you're a vegetarian then you're unlucky" — she laughed lightly.

I took the glass filled with cold drink and sat back and I said "No I guess I am lucky this time at least". And I smiled. And took one of the nuggets and quickly grabbed it and started to chew and trust me they were delicious.

"So 'Miss' why were you astonished to hear Calcutta"? If you don't mind can you ask you that?"

"Ha haha"! giggling— "Actually, I am a Bengali. So I thought you are from Calcutta!"........

"You are a Bong?????????????????????? Really?? Seriously?? You are ??" — I was a little shocked.

"Ha hahahaha!! Control yourself ! Lol yes I am a bong. Why Roy's are Punjabi or what?" She laughed out of sarcasm.

"Yes, Bengali girls whom I have come across are dark, have huge eyes and are a little plump" — I explained.

"Ha haha!! Not everyone is the same"— she replied.

I took the glass of cold drink and was observing her rings; none of them look like an engagement ring. She wore a diamond ring but she wore it in the middle finger of her right hand and the ring finger was not occupied and so I was very happy. And we started talking and after a while. Her phone was buzzing continuously. The messages I guess. They were continuous and after a while her phone started buzzing and she kept it aside. It buzzed at least three times and she kept it beside and now I think it was on silent because there was no buzzing now. And I was happy that she is talking to me my Aisha is talking to only me. But my mind was working (it has always the secriss-cross thoughts) was it her boyfriend calling her? Obviously, it's her boyfriend because no one will call a girl so many times. My heart sank and I thought of leaving.

"Aisha! I must leave now it is very late" — I said.

"Why so early? It is just 10 pm! (Not that she was falling for me she was actually a dude and girl with that friendly gene in her not like other girls who are shy and introvert. She was a friend, like I was talking to my best friend with no made-up things. She was pure. She was the purest thing. She is the purest person and the most beautiful girl by looks and by soul. I never thought that this rude girl can have such a gentle heart. I told you she is the only Flower in the paradise.

"Yeah yeah" (sounding serious). You have to go a long way na! I know you should leave now!" — And she busted out in a huge laugh.

"Ha ha" — you are hilarious!

"Bye Aisha good night"— I wished her and laughed out loud and started walking towards the door.

"Ha ha ha!!!" She was still laughing. "haha— Good night Varun Go safely" she added and laughed again.

Her smile is a special smile for me, and just me. An easy, natural grin that is pure and simple— like sunshine through a raindrop.

She smiled like she was surprised she remembered how.

Her smile sweetened the very air in my lungs.

Her smile was with all of herself.

The corners of her lips hooked themselves to my heart.

Always tentative, her smile would ease onto her face.

With immense purity and beautiful lace.

It was 12:45 am. I was in my room after I returned from Aisha's house I was lying on my bed flat facing the blank ceiling and was thinking of the meeting that took place. But from everything which was pricking me the most was the phone call that she didn't receive. Why Aisha did not pick up the phone? Who was calling her? Was it her boyfriend? Or anyone is disturbing her? Or she is already in love with someone or she is not? I was thinking all these when……………..

"Triiiiiiiiiiiiiiiiiiinnnnnnnnnnnnnn"

I received a phone call from an unknown number. I quickly received it hoping it was Aisha calling her.

"Hello?"— I said expecting a sweet voice from the other end.

"Bastard, what are you doing?" — A manly voice.

"Oh Golu! It's you" — I said killing my excitement.

"What happened to you? Are you all fine? — He replied back this time seriously.

"Nothing re. I am Ok just a little stressed." — I replied back (Hiding my feelings).

"You are sounding too low brother! Tell me what is it?" — He queried again.

"You are reaching day after tomorrow. If I am not wrong? You come then we will talk." I replied and disconnected the phone and lay down on my bed thinking about Aisha. Dizziness spells threatened to drop me to my knees and I felt my stomach contract and the sphincter muscle started to relax relax, a symptom of fight or flee, creating an even greater fear of messing myself.

The phone rang again and I hate dit for the fact of not leaving me alone when I want to. I awake to the dots of sunshine dancing across my room through the lace of my curtains. The aroma of honeysuckle is making its way through my open window from the vine outside. I can hear movement downstairs as my mom and dad prepare breakfast. As I look outside, the vast blue sky meets the rolling green hills, and I can see my four cows grazing in the open pasture. Oh God! It is morning. I jumped from my bed and checked out the time it was 10 am. I abused myself for getting late. I was hurrying myself and was rushing to the bathroom to get ready. Then...

"Why are you hurrying? Where are you going?" — Mom asked.

"OFFICE MOM"!! I almost shouted.

"You have office on a bank holiday?"— She protested.

"Oh yeah, Today is a holiday! Thank you mumma!" — I said and hugged her.

She tapped me and went on doing her household work. I got lethargic and went to the living room where my mom was sitting and doing her household stuffs. I was surfing the channels on the television and there was nothing interesting so I thought to go out with one of my colleague. So texted him for going out and have some fun and some booze of course. Just when I texted him for making a plan. My Mom said "We have to go for a wedding tonight. So don't take any *pans*" — putting the coriander leaves in a bowl and going towards the kitchen.

"Mom I am not going to any wedding I have already some plans. I will be out with my friends."— I argued.

"I didn't ask you, I am telling you that you have to come because it's important to come and socialise. You can have fun your Smoke (She exaggerated) Later." — She snapped and left the room.

I texted back my colleague and told him to cancel as I have got some work. It is super crap and I hate this. I knew it was one of our organisation's members wedding so I knew a few people who will come and I could survive with those. I quickly called Ritu who is a cute girl and in her early twenties but a kid to me whom I treat her like a sister and John who was of my age and a spoiled and an irritating guy who is always in front of his computer screen and playing games. I confirmed and they were pretty excited about the gathering today and I was not. But someone I have to talk to at least. I had a good sleep throughout the afternoon with a good heavy lunch and I was relaxed. Mom shook me up to wake up it was 6:49 pm and we were leaving by 8:00 pm and for that I have to get ready and look good of course.

I checked my phone *six messages received*!!!!

Four from John—

1. Where are you?
2. Ritu is really coming?
3. I am standing alone.
4. Where the hell are you?

2. from Ritu— where are you *bhaiya*? I am on the way.

And I replied to both of them and replied "coming". I quickly got up went from a shower and changed myself into a black shirt with camel colour trousers and black ankle shoes which looked terrific. I settled my hair with some gel and water and I was looking cool. Yeah !!!

I took the car out and peeped into Aisha's garage she wasn't there but her car was. It feels it has been ages I haven't seen her. I drove the car to Hotel Regency where the wedding was taking place. My parents went inside and I parked the car and were going in. I just went inside and I could see Ritu and John coming towards me.

"Why are you so late?" They asked.

"Actually I slept off "— I replied. And John wasn't bothered because he liked Ritu and she was there with him and I was feeling jealous (No, No not because of Ritu). I was missing my Aisha. I also wanted her to be with me by my side. But she doesn't even know that someone loves her. I envy John he has his love and my love? When they were talking I should say flirting to each other I was looking out the place of how it is decorated. Indian weddings are very bright events, filled with ritual and celebration, which continue for several days. The entrance has the shenaiwala who was playing the usual bridal tune. The stage which was at the end of the huge lawn was decorated by white and red roses and some purple orchids which were beautiful. There was a long row for stalls which was on the other side and was properly placed. They are not small affairs, often with 400-1000 people attending (many of whom are unknown to the bride and groom). Though most marriages are arranged, some couples in urban areas have love marriages. The true Indian wedding is about two families getting wedded socially with much less emphasis on the individuals involved. We all went to the stage where the important person for the day was sitting yep the groom in his golden and white *sherwani* and he was looking good. We congratulated him and came back to basic with me, Ritu and John. All the guests were well dressed, the kids were hoping from one place to other and the young ones like us were eyeing to one another and the middle age people I mean all the oldies were just eating. They were least interested in the wedding but more interested for the food and their varieties. And some guests were clicking pictures on the stage with a plastic smile (I hate the most).

"*Bhaiya*? Where are you lost?"—Asked Ritu querying me with her big round eyes.

"Nothing nothing at all"— I replied and realised actually I was lost (Aisha you are not allowing me to breathe without you. Aisha I love you). I said this to me not in front of them. Ha haha !

We three were chatting and teasing the oldies and checking out that they were only here to eat. We were standing near the entrance because it was the only place which was less crowded and that was chosen by Ritu and obviously where Ritu is John is in the same direction. I really don't know whether John is seriously in love with Ritu or he is just flirting. I was sipping my black cola (reminded me of Aisha and the chat last night with her). I realised I didn't notice any girl tonight in the wedding and that was weird for me because this never happened. I was changing. And I was chatting with passing a few fake smiles to the others whom I know somehow don't know why. Was I in my conscious or I was thinking too much or was it real or it was just an illusion. I could see a fade image of a human which was coming close to the entrance. It was becoming clearer as the few seconds passed and my eyes didn't blink. For a person whose eyes were strained with the umknown crowd in marriage it was a pleasant sight. She was wearing a yellow suit which was near her ankles and had a beautiful fall with big pink embroidered flowers on the borders. She wore no makeup just a touch of kohl on her eyes yet her beauty was touching the pinnacle of charm and her long silky hair and radiant charm in her face. Yep, it was Aisha!!!!!!!!!!!

And I lost in my thoughts with the sound of violins and the melody of song breaking the silence of the strange world. I go along be my love I only can think. Her hair falling till her waist a little curl at the end was adhering more to her beauty. She was holding the arm of a man in an elegant style like she was a princess; the old man was in his late forties who were wearing an exclusive shirt which had red thin stripes on a black shirt. Her mere presence makes my world a place worth living of pleasure immense. That's the kind of joy she brings to the world of mine. She walked with the old man and entered the lawn and got into the crowd, but I could see her completely. As I can only see her. Only her.....

When you love someone,

You forget the world

Whilst her love makes you forget even you,

I ask nothing but love and is always true.

"Varun !!Varun"?? Bro I am calling you for so long where are you lost? Are you ok?— John shook me and said.

"Your phone is ringing"— John added.

"No No!! Hold Varun *bhaiya* now!! Else he will fall for that girl wearing a yellow suit" — Ritu jumped out of excitement and laughed out loud.

"Shut up you two. Nothing like that. I was just......"

"You were just"???????— They teased together.

And I was blushing and my heart was pumping to my head and then to my knees. I was just looking at her I got hypnotised.

Wondering how someone can look so fine,

And when it comes to colours you wear

Every dress looks perfect making you dear

While eyes you have has sparkling glow

Seeing them can make any heartbeat slow

Your smile is so cheerful if watched from close

Can heal any wound if given as dose

Your lips are somehow whitish pink

This makes the viewer skip his blink

When it comes to hair so maintained

Every word of praise remains unexplained!

I got back to my consciousness all because of the stupid John and Ritu's conversation; because Ritu was starving, and John was after her. They called me to eat with them but I wanted to see Aisha and because of these two my Aisha was lost in the crowd. So, I followed them and filled my plate and sat down on a round table and then leaving the two love birds I went to fetch a water bottle for myself and.......

****CLASH****

"YOU??????????" — Exclaimed Aisha !!!!

"What are you doing here"?? — Elatedly, asked Aisha.

"Hi Aisha! How are you? It is my friend's wedding"— I replied (and you look magnificent) I said this to myself (not to her. Shall I tell her now? Later?)

"Tell me about it. It is your friend's weding and you are eating like guests here?" Are you kidding me? And you are not even boozing?" — Her beautiful eyes were almost popping out because of excitement when — Aisha said.

"Ssshhhhhhhhhhhh Aisha.... People are going to kill us here only...If they listen to the word booze" — I replied and trying to make her calm.

"He he he!!!"— She giggled.

"And you are here?" — I asked (and realised I haven't had a bite from my plate and it was lying there on the table. Forget everything Aisha is with me. What say? :)

"I am with my parents here. Don't know whose wedding it is but I am here"— : she gave me a beautiful smile".

"Thank god you are here I was so bored" — Aisha said.

She wanted my company. Actually, she loves my company that is why she wants me with her. And I wanted to jump in the air click my feet and say "YABA DABA DOO" like FRED FLINSTONES.

"Why were you so excited about the booze thing?" — I asked (thinking of starting a new conversation)

"Ha haha!Actuallyyyy.....(she paused). I thought a man who's aged around 25 to 26 and he doesn't booze so that was a shock to me!" — She has a complete expression on her face that she was confused about my age.

"Twenty five!!! I replied and she laughed out really loud and I haven't seen a smile like hers'. The most innocent SMILE!!!!! She was gentle she was pure she was a girl who's energetic, outgoing, happy, optimistic, always in a good mood and spunky.

Her simple smile, lights my heart a blaze.

The shine of pearl sends my mind into a daze.

It's only a smile to you,

but to me it makes my world so new.

"Varun!!!!! Someone bellowed"— it wasn't Aisha. It was Noooooo..................... not now!! It was John and Ritu.

"Where did you disappear? We have been searching for you?" — Curious John but winked.

I introduced Aisha to John and Ritu and she gave them the fakest of smiles and the most elitist look. She stood there for a few minutes and I think she waited for them to leave. But asshole John never left. Aisha wished me good night and left the place.

Soon there breathed a wind on me,

Nor sound no motion made:

Its path was not upon the sea,

In ripple or in shade.

I came home and I had four shots of whiskey (without water just wanted you to know how much drunk I was. I was lost in her. I was in love with her.

I was listening to romantic songs,

Which I never knew how did it long,

I was amazed with my own tune,

Aisha is what I was as my Fortune.

I was lying on my bed (again) flat and listening to the songs and thinking of only Aisha. I stood up tried to control myself. I stood in front of the mirror. I had a feeling of my t-shirt getting wet and slowly I couldn't see myself in the mirror. No I wasn't dozing off, tears rolled from my eyes and touched my cheeks.

When the burning moment breaks,

And all things are out of mind,

And only joy of battle takes

By the throat and makes him blind.

I was CRYING!!!!!!!!!

It was 6:30 am and I woke up pretty early. Today I woke up pretty early (way too early). It was a quiet morning and after a hot night yes Gwalior's hot nowadays it was really refreshing. Sun had risen but it was mild so it was quite cool and I went out to my terrace with the chilly morning breeze greeting me. I saw the children from the neighbourhood cricket summer camp playing to become tomorrow's Sachin, Sourav, Dravid. The sounds of the boys with a background score provided by cuckoos, Indian *mynas* (strangely I see crows and sparrows the most common birds) delighted me. Seeing those little boys I was lost into my own childhood when summer vacation was a real fun and in the early morning. I was happy today because it was Friday and my Best friend Golu was coming after a year and this made me feel ecstatic. The weather was the woodland trees that stood together; they stand to them each one a friend. They gently speak in the windy weather. They guide to Valley and ridge's end. I stood amazed when an angel with an invisible halo and wings was sitting on the terrace on the wooden chair wearing a tank top which was white in colour and a pink Capri sport and hair was tied into a rough bun and she was looking sexy. But I sensed an air of desperation surround her, like a heavy cloak that she was tired of carrying. It was evident in her crystal eyes as they darted about looking for friendly territory; a friendly face with whom she could sit and feel safe and at ease with. It was evident in the way she struggled to breathe as her chest heaved up and down and she - she - trying so hard to keep it under control.

Saving mental conversations with figments, to even notice that she existed. And I felt for her.

She sat for a while distracting herself by looking at the birds on the tree — I'm sure a futile attempt of stilling her overwrought mind— her legs jitterbugging the time away.

As I came close to her; I continued looking at her face. It was a face that carried the scars of a hard life within its young crevices. Away from prying eyes she at last crumpled to the floor, finally taking off the cloak that covered her distress. And it was then that I saw the tears pour freely from her eyes. It was then that I saw the pain that lived within in its full rawness.

No, this was not something birthed from a fear of clouds. This was something else; something deeper, something that affected the visceral. And this young woman — sad, distressed, and in deep emotional pain—had found a conduit on which to lay the blame. And I felt for her.

And I watered it in fears,

Her morning was with deep tears,

And I was stunned with her usual smiles,

And with soft deceitful wiles.

I have never seen her sad, although she is always so cheerful no one can ever think she has something inside her that can make her sad. I was struck there. Why is my Aisha sad? I was wondering for the whole day. What is there inside her? It isn't because of a fight with family or friends. It is something deep. Deeper then I can ever think. But that pure smile with lots of charm and sweetness? Was that fake? Well was she really fake? Her eyes, her Black eyes expressed her, the more captivating it is to just stare at them. Her eyes don't always resemble water, but they do resemble this deep pool of 'look at me', and 'I'm innocent'. Her eyes were more sensitive then I have ever seen. And when they smile, there's nothing to beat it. No!! It cannot be. She cannot be fake! There is something in her which is making her sad because,

A sin the sudden, deep pain in her heart was so bad, she felt like her whole world had come crashing down on her, and she collapsed to her knees sobbing in her distress. Glee tear rolled down her cheek.

She shouldn't have been crying, but she was too numb to even think about crying.

I can do nothing except to just think about that precious pearl of tear which was dropping from her innocent eyes.

It was 6:59 pm, I was right on-time to pick up my best friend Golu from the station his actual name is (Mayur) but I call him Golu as it's his pet name. I came to office in my dad's car today as I had to pick up Golu from the station and he is also a child and my brother for my parents. They love him more than me. I started the car and the weather outside was awesome the wind was blowing nicely and some droplets were flickering on my and on the wind screen and then a slow romantic song Everything I do I do it for you.

"I love rains and I love Aisha" — I smiled and said to myself.

I reached the platform after parking the car in the parking area and the time was 7:15 pm. There was squealing of train's brakes. A 'trundle' sound when the train which was on platform number 1 starts to move away. A slightly burnt smell from the brakes, A 'jingle' when an announcement is about to be made. A muffled announcement was made about train boarding or delays and reminding people not to touch bags which are unattended. There was chatter amongst all the passengers who were either getting ready to board the incoming train or they just got down from other train and are rushing home. In India, everyday and everyone is in a rush. May I have your attention please. Train No.12121- Shatabdi express which is coming from Bhopal is shortly arriving on platform No.1.... and it was repeated. Sound of people dragging themselves in a rush along those suitcases on wheels. Little children running round playing tag waiting for the train to come and the other and people chatting. I was happy. My heart was smiling my best friend was coming to me in just few minutes.

Six- feet tall like a thin bark of a tree who was wearing a sky blue T-shirt very thin and was wearing a low waist jeans which looked it will just about to fall but it never did; and a big black backpack and a water bottle of Aquafina in his hand. He jumped from the door of the train and hugged me and we both were very happy not happy I was ecstatic. We hugged each other stood there and didn't speak to each other for a moment.

"Bro!!!!!!!!!! You are here!!!!" — I enthusiastically said.

"Give me your bag" — I added.

"Areeee.... I am not your girl friend, hold this"— he handed me over a Frooti bottle and said to have it. He didn't have it because he knew I love Frooti:

Never seek to tell his friend love

Love that never said can be;

For the gentle and sweet gesture

Silently, invisibly my friend has love for me.

We reached home and he was sitting in my room after having dinner with my parents and we were chatting and having a humorous evening after a long time. We were together; he was wearing a white colour T- shirt and brown boxers and sitting near the window of my room on a cushion stool and lighting up his cigarette by keeping his cigarette at the corner of his lips and fumigating it.

"You have a day off tomorrow?" — Golu asked (there was something going on in his head).

"I love Aisha"— I was straight as I said (I could not hide my feelings anymore. I wanted someone so that I can talk my heart out and there was no one better than Golu so I snapped).

Earlier, Golu was looking out of the window and not making any eye contact when we were talking but as soon as I snapped about Aisha! He was shocked. He stood up and was shocked......!

"What???" — He was shocked completely.

"You are in Love??? Are you kidding me"— He replied.

He was actually traumatised. He looked up at me and I just nodded my head and looked down.

"OH MY GOD"!!!!! You are in love....!!!" — He said (his eyes were popping out and was shaken he was rubbing his head and pulling his hair and smiling)

"I never thought you will ever fall in love"— He added.

"I thought the same but .... " — I paused.

"Who is the Girl? That Aisha?" — He enquired.

"Yes!!!"

"She is the one bro; she is the one I cannot live without. She is the one I want to spend my whole life with her. She is the................"

"TRINNNNNNNNNNNNNNNNNNNNNN" — (Sometimes phones should be banned for a certain amount of time when I was discussing the most important phase of my life-disgusting).

His Samsung white phone was lying on my bed and he asked me to look at the phone for him as to who it was it. It was "Winnie calling"...

Winnie is Golu's childhood friend. They are actually the nappy friends. I haven't seen a boy and a girl can be such real good friends they are friends forever. They both can be the example of a boy and a girl can be the best of friends he is better friend to her than me and sometimes it hurts me but I am fine because my friend is happy. Though I haven't met Winnie but I have heard a lot about her.

"Hellllllllllllllllllllllllllllllooooooooooooooooooooooooooooo"— Golu stretched hello as he answered the phone.

"Aree... But..... Listen....wait....First......Ok....Listen....." — Golu stammered (He sounded too funny)

Ha hahahaha ! — he laughed out loud.

"Ok will meet up tomorrow in the evening." — He replied and disconnected (so this implies Winnie is in Gwalior itself).

"Now, tell me about Aisha. He quickly came near me and sat down"— he asked curiously.

"Good night I am going off to sleep. You phone call ruined up the flow of my feelings. Will talk about it later" — I said and soaked my head into my pillow and was lying straight on my bed. He shook me and kicked me and made me sit again.

"She's beautiful, She's beautiful.: I sang it like "You are beautiful" (LOL)

"Her eyes are jet black with black flecks though out the irises. Looking into them was comparable to staring at a vast and clear ocean. The curve of her nose was smooth and seamless as if her face had been built only to support such a perfect structure."

The moonlight danced across her fair skin, her high cheekbones highlighted from the soft light. Her mocha brown eyes stared out beneath delicate eyebrows, and a wave of ebony hair cascaded around her shoulders. Her lips were full and pink, perfectly proportioned; as was the pointed nose above them. Her flawless skin accentuated the beauty of her slender visage. And if you talk about purity I haven't seen a girl like her in my life throughout, and you also know I have met so many girls but this girl is formed of purity. She is an amazing human being, she laughs with her whole heart and she's intelligent as well she looks after a whole business. But there is something that she is all sad. I want to know her what is making her sad and I want to erase all her worries and make her happy, not happy, the happiest person on earth.

"But how do you know she's sad?" — Golu asked with a cold voice.

"I know"— I just answered without giving any sort of explanation.

"When are you going to tell her"? — He asked before I could finish my sentence.

"When I will get to know she is not committed".— I gazed at Golu.

"You don't even know that if she is even single?" — He was amazed.

"Let's sleep. I hope it is not like your other flings" — Golu snapped.

"I Love her" — I snapped and shouted at Golu. And now Golu got the answer of how was I feeling.

"You know what it is like if you ever put your arms out and spin really, really fast? That's what love is like. It makes your heart race. It turns the world upside down. But if you're not careful, if you don't keep your eyes on something still, you can lose your balance. You can't see what's happening to the people around you. You can't see that you're about to fall".

"Love, like truth and beauty, is concrete. Love is not fundamentally a sweet feeling; not, at heart, a matter of sentiment, attachment, or being drawn toward. Love is active, effective, a matter of making reciprocal and mutually beneficial relation with one's friends and enemies." — I replied like I was reading out philosophy of love from some book. (I realised then I really said all this). Golu stood amazed and gazed at me for some time and then we both went off to sleep. Not we (I was just lying on my bed and thinking of just Aisha and her tears of what was making her sad. Earlier I used to think of my work how to make it better but now that bottled glass eyed my boss doesn't irritates me, I think it not like that it just I am just too involved about Aisha).

I will make you brooches and toys for your delight,

Of bird song at morning and star shine at night,

I shall be the music when no one else is near,

A fine song for singing and a rare song to hear.

It was the 6th of July, 2013 and it was Richa's birthday (Richa is Golu's girlfriend and she lives in Gwalior and she doesn't know that Golu has come to Gwalior) and now I just called her and wished her on her birthday and she complained that my best friend has forgot her birthday and she was sobbing and I gave her confidence that he hasn't he is busy in a meeting in office and now I demanded her to come to the fort to meet me because she was a good friend to me as well but she denied because she was upset but then I requested and then she agreed (Girls and their tantrums I tell you, but without them they are incomplete as well :). And our plan was that Golu and I....... Oh wait.... Read below : ha hahaha !!

After her tantrums and her unexplained excuses we dressed in our jeans and T's respectively. I was wearing a black jeans and a mauvepolo T-shirt and Golu was wearing the military green trousers and a black plain shirt. And I took the car out (dad left it for us).

We were driving through the steep road of the Gwalior fort. Steeped in the splendorous of its past a successful transition into a modern Indian city, vibrant and bursting. Gwalior fort dominates the city and its most magnificent monuments. A steep road winds up towards the road, flanked by statues of Jain tirthankaras carved into the rock face. The fort stands up unite and is conical in shape and is built on a solitary hillock. The rock formations of hill fort through horizontally placed strata forms almost a perpendicular precipice. The weather was filled with emotions like the sun and dark grey clouds were making love. Sometimes the clouds were glittering and sometimes and sun was hiding its rays from us. It was a beautiful weather there were sometimes sprinkles of water which were adding a magical feeling in the atmosphere. We sat on a stair which was the top most place from where the whole of Gwalior was visible and it looked tiny as the playhouses which we used to play in our childhood.

"Richa Calling"— Golu exclaimed (That's my phone dude).

I received her call and she called me to inform me that she had reached the fort and she was coming to the place where we were sitting. Golu made signs while I was talking to her (he was trying to say something that I couldn't understand) he ran and hid behind a huge rock. Golu was now sneaking behind the huge stone. I could see a fade image of a girl which was coming near and I could make out that she was Richa. A sweet and a very simple looking girl with a tanned skin, a healthy golden-brown tint with an oval face with big eyes petite nose and big and pouty lips which were coloured in deep pink. Hair was curly and was ending till her shoulders as they were open. She was wearing a pink kurti and a pair of pink slacks and she was coming towards me with a smile on her face but with confused eyes. She came near me and I wished her birthday..................

"Happy birthday" — A young man hugged her tightly from her back and they hugged each other like souls being together as one. They kissed each other on their lips and I was sitting there, who shifted his eyes to the other corner and changed my place so that I could give them all their space in serene. I missed Aisha. I wish I could just be with her and hold her hand and sit with her in silence." Love is also the great healer. It heals conflict, hatred, and injustice and as Martin Luther King Junior said, "Darkness cannot drive out darkness; only light can do that. Hate cannot drive out hate; only love can do that".

As I was thinking about Aisha they went on with their romance and Golu opened up a carton box which had a Black Forest Cake– Chocolate crème cake with cherries, chocolate mousse and triple section, whip cream frosting and chocolate crumbles on the sides. It looked delicious and I was starving and the cake looked marvelous they were busy romancing I took the opportunity and filled my tummy with that yummy cake.

"So where is the party tonight dude?" — I asked adding humour, (though I know there was no party at all but we should confirm it. What say? Who will not want another chance of having such delicious cake and some booze to personify the treasure :D)

"Well we will go out for dinner" — Richa replied sweetly.

"Ummmmmm… I have a better plan" — (Golu replied creating mystery)

"Hmmmm… How about Central Park — Spectrum the disco at seven pm sharp" — He questioned and announced.

"Dude that would be wonderful" — I jumped and I in a jovial mood : replied him.

"But if not booked before it cannot be done"— I added regaining my consciousness. "Some as shole must have booked before".

"Yeah true, and That asshole is Mayur (Golu)" — he said and looked into Richa's eyes.

"Whaaaaatt....."???? Richa was flabbergasted totally shocked her eyes were out and she was standing strong as rock and there wears-tears flowing like a waterfall with a smiling face who hugged Golu and stood there for a few moments. (Golu is an awesome human being anyone would fall for him and these gestures are amazing if I were a girl I would have fallen as well but I am not a girl so get up).

It was 6:47 pm and getting ready for the party actually meant getting ready more for the booze. He hehe!! I was wearing a white shirt with a black strip in the button area and was wearing a light blue jeans add on with navy blue colour Zara shoes! I was brushing my hair in front of the mirror and Golu was checking money in his wallet and tying his shoes later.

"Hola! I am looking great.." — I winked at Golu and gave him a smirk.

"Yeah yeah you to look like a hero and you are waiting for the girls in the party so many girls will come and hit on you. Yeah right?" — He smiled and winked at me.

"Sorry Dude but you are forgetting I am a one women man" — I gazed at Golu and replied and he smiled back at me. "We are getting late. Let's go" — I added.

After getting late we forgot that we have to pick up Richa too. (Gosh I forgot the birthday girl ha ha ha). After picking up Richa we reached the hotel right away and we were not that late only by 45 minutes. Ha haha!! (Let me describe to you about the Birthday Girl Richa to you).

Richa was wearing a magenta colour long top with a black tight legging with black footwear's which were covered. Her eyes were made up with a grey eye shadow and hint of kohl and a deep pink lipstick. She was looking nice but not like my Aisha.

The party started and guests were coming in, the music was loud and the bar is in full swing, and floating rounds of cocktails permeate the garden outside, until the air is alive with chatter and laughter, and casual innuendo and introductions forgotten on the spot, and enthusiastic meetings between women who never knew each other's names. An evening of truly delicious *hor-d'oeuvers*, finger food and splendid aperitifs awaits you. Topped off with desserts to place on everyone's palate. Dancing, it is often said, is the visible and creative expression of the body's natural movements. (Not in my case I guess I dance insanely and girls used to die on my dancing) 'wink' it is a fun way to cut loose and celebrate the joys of life. And nowhere is this *joie de vivre* celebrated in grandeur style than in not at all a fun city. From live music to late night, The Beach on Bourbon.... Brass band throw downs, electronic music bashes. I was drooling as I was very high and not interested in any of the girl where the crowd was of thirty people including girls and boys. I was on the dance floor I was dancing but all of a sudden my head wobbled and I wondered what I was viewing was true was actually there or I was hallucinating?

As I walked down across the dance floor to the entrance, a small blur suddenly dived in front of me. For a moment all I could see was frothy pink fabric and lace, and then time seemed to slow. The blur focussed into a young girl. Her long black hair was curled into loose ringlets and framed a round sweet and cute shaped face with a sharp nose and Cupid's bow lips. Her blue eyes met mine; we stood looking at each other for a moment, and then she flashed me a sparkling smile, her whole person lighting up with it. With that she turned away and continued her dash through the streets, her Lolita style dress flying behind her. She was talking to Golu. (Was I dreaming).

"Winnie! He is Varun — Golu introducing me to Aisha.

"Winnie or Aisha"??? — I was confused.

"Ha ha! Both Varun" — Aisha giggled.

"Ok, so you guys have met before" — Golu ogled at me and handed over a glass of Martini to Aisha.

"AISHA"?????? Right???" — I confirmed.

"Ha haha Varun" — Yes Aisha!!! :You are right don't worry that's just my nick name" — she smiled.

She was an angel who sat upon the bosom,

Under a cloud of her hair

And her pink lips sang them a pure song,

Till stars grew out of the air.

Golu left and I was sitting with Aisha, My Aisha. She was sipping her Martini and watching the crowd on the dance floor all the boys were eyeing her and I gave all of them a strong look and gave them a hint that don't stare at her. I was pretty high and I wanted them to blast their faces but controlled as I just wanted to hold hands with Aisha and talk to her for hours.

"Aisha, May I dance with you"? — I asked and I was too direct.

"Sorry Varun! But I don't dance actually I can't dance" — she replied.

"You look beautiful" — I was immediate and honest.

"Really? Lol! Hey Thanks"— She replied cutely and added her charming style to it. (She was blushing).

She danced with Golu (she never danced with me because I think I was still a stranger to her but she was my soul now). They danced like they both were still in kindergarten and they actually acted that ways.

She's a baby!

She's a Blossom!

She's a rare flower!

The party ended after all the dance and music and the short flings which happen in every party and the show off their respective dresses of the females gathered and I can bet all envied my Aisha including the birthday girl. We dropped Richa home and I was freaking smashed and I couldn't remember the time what time it was but Golu was shouting that his train was in sometime. (I could sense that).

As soon as Golu dropped Richa to her place, he came and sat in the car and the first thing he said was "Dude you are not meeting Aisha anymore" — Golu snapped.

"You mean Aisha?" — I said with my blotto voice and my stoned eyes.

"Yes dude Aisha, listen dude she is my best friend and I in any case I don't want her to get hurt and I will not tolerate any tears. And dude I know her and I know you" — Golu snapped.

"She is a very sensitive girl; she is not the girl whom she shows herself out. She is... She is like a baby" — Golu explained.

"Bro!!!! I will just say one thing without her I am incomplete and I want to spend the rest of my life with her"— I gripped.

We both gazed at each other for a while and Golu ended up saying "Take care!!!"

When words are less and feelings are high

When knowledge is more and senses that go,

This is man's perdition to get live,

When for the love he ought to die.

The entry platform had tea stalls, book stalls and a few shops of cold drinks, fruits and children toys. Some push - carriages are moving hurriedly on the platforms. Many vendors are selling different eatables sliced bread pakoras, biscuits, packaged foods and other things. And smaller stations there are periods of "almost nothing" when no train is arriving, leaving, or stopping at the station. There will be freight trains coming through, usually with an announcement for passengers to step back and pay attention. Trains are announced (and in case of delays, there is one announcement at the time when the train should arrive and another when it actually comes).

When a train comes in you hear the locomotive, the wheels, the brakes with a hiss and squeak, the doors (manual or pneumatic) - then an announcement to board the train, a whistle, sometimes a warning sound from the doors, then the sound of passenger schmoozing and of the train slowly rolling out. Yes, we were at the station at about three in the morning because Golu was leaving for Bangalore tonight. Golu left and I was again lonely. On my way home it was raining heavily; Gwalior had never these monsoon days but I was wondering of the only thing that was wobbling in my head was "Take care". Take care? Was that for me? Or Aisha? Or my feelings I couldn't understand. I was back home legless and I lay straight to my bed and I was thinking of Aisha. God made us meet and he's making us meet every time (God I never thought I will say such types of things I used to laugh at such type of statements.. omg … let's continue what you guys say? ;)

I was sloshed but then again I took up my wine bottle and took a wine glass and soared towards the terrace. Love creates righteousness, or justice, here on earth. To make love is to make justice. As advocates and activists for justice know, loving involves struggle, resistance, risk. For this reason loving involves commitment. We are not automatic lovers of self, others, world, or God. Love does not just happen. We are not love machines, puppets on the strings of a deity called love. Love is a choice – not simply, or necessarily, a rational choice, but rather a willingness to be present to others without pretense or guile. And what I was looking was my alcohol making me see or was it real. Or I could see what I actually wanted? If I get her in my life I will leave each and everything just because of her just because of my Aisha my love of my life. She was actually there (I guess) sitting on the terrace slab of both the joins of our terrace. She wore a white spaghetti top which showed her most of her skin but she wasn't looking vulgar she looked absolutely graceful and adding a red shorts which had white sheep's all over her shorts which looked incredibly cute and she was having a tub of ice cream I think it was chocolate from the colour I could make out. She was looking up at the sky and wondering something or asking some questions from up there. I really don't know. (She was sitting with her back to me so she didn't know that I was there and just looking at her). She slightly turned her head and A sin the sudden, deep pain in her heart was so bad, she felt like her whole world had come crashing down on her, and she collapsed to her knees sobbing in her distress tear rolled down her cheek. She should have been crying, but she was too numb to even think about crying. Her eyes were big and a pretty shade of hazel. They had a gleam to them, like a mastermind. Dreamingly? Intelligence? Anyways, something intense was happening in her head right now, I nearly didn't want to approach her, it would be a shame to disturb but I saw a tear from her beautiful eyes and I couldn't see that.

"Aisha what happened why are you crying"? — I summoned as I felt miserable.

She quickly removed her tear from her right hand and looked at me and gave me a fake smile.

"Nothing at all" — she denied

"Why are you crying? Are you Ok?" — I repeated. My heart sank to see her cry. I kept my glass and the wine bottle on the small wooden table which was structured by me on my terrace. She was sitting and I was standing and looking at her with my hands on my waist and I was ready to break the person's face that made my love cry.

"Nothing re. Just like that. Just some memories which come and directly hit me" — she replied.

"But you looked so happy in the party I was so happy to see you happy and dancing like a kid" — I was honest and was trying to make her console.

"Alcohol hits the emotional trigger. You know na!" — She winked at me and smiled.

She sat on the slab with her legs folded and with the chocolate bucket in her hand. (Yep, it was chocolate see I was right. I am always right when the things comes to Aisha)

"Are you sure"? — I confirmed.

"Yeah yeah! Relax. Come sit"— she flapped her palm on the long slab where she was sitting opposite to her which have an indication me to sit there on the slab in front of her. (I was happy)

"You want to have some ice-cream?" — She offered.

"I am sure you love ice-cream"! — I demanded as I was sure like the way she was having it.

"Ha haha — I hate ice cream, I hate sweets!" — She replied back looking down at her tub.

"Huh? What? Then why are you having these" — I was astonished.

"Desserts are opposite to stressed so trying to make my emotions light" — "have it" — she ordered.

"You want to have some?" — I showed her my wine bottle and asked her.

"Man you have wine, Red wine"? obviously yaar!! — She replied with excitement. "I love red wine" — she added.

"Wait let me go and fetch another glass. I will come in no minute" — I quickly ran.

I really came up in no time and poured red wine in two of the glasses and gave one to her and held it and said cheers!!! She had a sip of her wine glass and kept it near her and again looked up at the sky.

"Aisha why are you sad"? — I directly enquired.

She turned up to me, explored me and said nothing but a smile!

I could feel there is something in her heart. Aisha's eyes were an open window; although that is true for everyone, it is also true that a girl can really show more emotion than a guy could. She smiles with her eyes, express sadness, fear, anger. I felt like her heart had been ripped out.

"Aisha you can tell it to me. I am your friend" — I said sensitively.

"Friend! He he! Nice! Thanks Varun" — she replied.

"Why did you laugh? What was there to laugh? I genuinely said that". — I said angrily.

"You know Varun. Life is not about whom you were, it is all about who you are and the person you have the potential to be! That's all is life." — Aisha replied.

The first the Annunciation;

The second the visitation;

The third the consolation.

Of human that's the repetition.

Aisha recited.

I was astonished and freaking delighted to hear what she said — I was sure what it was written on her own. I was pretty much impressed.

"So miss Aisha. The girl who loves to party, loves wine, hates desserts, loves dogs and loves the colour yellow"??

She was shocked to hear this and said — "Man how do you know that I love dogs and my favourite colour is yellow"???????

"A cute pretty girl hugged a roadside pup few months ago and now its name is 'Ronaldo'. She bends and took the pup in her arms and played with it and adored it. So, anybody could sense that!" — replied with a smile.

"Where were you? And you saw me that day?" — she was full in shock and which showed her round big eyes which were ready to pop out and she drank the full glass of wine.

"And how do you know my favourite colour is yellow"— she asked me inquisitively.

"A girl who has a YELLOW car, I think there is only one car in the city and that's obviously yours. You have a yellow wallet, you wear yellow shoes and you listen to songs like "Yellow" from Coldplay and right now you are wearing yellow slippers" — I described.

"Ha ha ha!!! That's fabulous! You are hilarious" — she said out of excitement. "That's so sweet"— she added.

"What are you doing tomorrow"? — I asked Aisha (alcohol gives you a lot of courage even)

"OMG!! Tomorrow is office again. I will not return before 7:30 pm" — she explained.

"Same here." — I replied.

"So, Mr. New Friend is asking me on a date" — she smiled at her best and was a hint of sarcasm.

"Actually (a=b=c) you are Golu's best friend and Golu is my best friend so we both are logically already friends." — I replied

"HA HAHAHAHAHAHAHA" — she laughed hard." What was that? hahaha! — you are crazy."— she replied.

"Ok cool! I will be ready by 7:45 pm and give you a call! Oh shit! Mr. Manager I don't have your number. Give it to me"! — She said. And I gave her my number and took hers and saved it in OFFICIALY.:

It was 3:30 pm and I was very happy and working at my office and waiting for 8:00 pm because it was official date with my Aisha. But still I had a sad feeling and wanted to know what the reason she was crying for was. Is she single? But that isn't affecting much too me as I had fallen in love with her and I never knew I will ever fall for anyone and that too so hard.

I was happy and gay and singing a slay

Phone got buzzed and said wassup

Aisha pinged and said on watsapp

Add me whenever you can do up

I got back home early today

Didn't told mom I am going with that bay

I texted her to come near the nearer shop

She said you pick me up because I cannot hop

I will take my car Aisha said

Whatever you say— I replied

She told at home she was going with me

I got confused weather I was he or a she

Reached Taj half-past eight

And she was looking glamorous, difficult to rate

She was wearing a short dress of black and grey

And I was wearing jeans black and looked like his slave

She ordered Chinese and a glass of red wine

I ordered the same but with JD in my hand

We spoke and spoke for hours and we were friends

She divided the money as it wasn't a date.

We meet once in a week

But never told about her weak

She was fun filled and full of life

But somewhere she is sad a slight

Her eyes speaks her inner feeling

I wish I was the one of her curing

She is not what she shows outside

She is pure person with a lot of disguise

She is unique in the box of crayons colour

I must say she is the one and only Rare Flower!!!

Weeks passed, months passed we got along really nicely and now we are good friends. Golu is though still concerned about mine and Aisha's meetings. But we are good friends, I never showed her that I was madly in love with her and she didn't even give me a hint about anything. She is actually a dude friend not the typical girls and their irritating tantrums she was "different". She liked me calling 'dodo' she loved the name indeed all other girls would have made a different scene regarding the whole but no she was not like the others. She was rude though hilarious; she was arrogant but used to laugh out loud in a quiet place and anyone couldn't do anything except staring. She drives at 120 km/hr when she's in "her" type of mood else she will drive at 20 km/hr and a cyclist can overtake her easily (this is true I have experienced this). She cries with huge drops of water but silently and then in a sudden will laugh out loud like nothing sad ever happened. She had a unique sense of dressing and a unique selection of clothes shoes and all accessories. She writes sometimes I have seen her writing but she never shared it with me. She had a secret desire that no one knew only Ronaldo (I told you she is hilarious) and the purest form on earth. She is a shopaholic I think the movie "confessions on a shopaholic was made on her". She has to shop every week else she falls sad and weak. She is short tempered had a huge anger and will throw stuffs anything which is nearby her, she recently broke a remote control, cordless phone and her mom's blackberry phone but in fifteen minutes her anger cools down and she took all of them and made repaired on her own and said sorry to her mother also and I was there sitting watching all this. She was angry because? I think she doesn't even remember. She can make a sudden plan and will put her hundred per cent to make it anyhow. She has ego and will forgive the person who has hurt her but never forget. If you are in love with this woman then be prepared to be very happy or be very sorry (but I am extremely happy). She is a very busy person with her own matters. She is able to live by herself without any guy in her life, a very strong person indeed. She thinks she could do anything that a man can do. She is a leader; a real confident type. She likes to do things by herself, such as serving herself, opening the door herself. Because she thinks waiting for a helping hand is a waste of time, and she is not patient enough to wait around for that. If she starts to ask you out, do not think she is starting to flirt with you, but because she thinks it is a waste of time to wait for you to be the one who asked. She likes a COOL guy who sometime acts like he is ignoring her, so he has a chance to show her his own confidence. Her appearance is beautiful as a rose. She is unpredictable and can give you an impression of smooth whipped cream, then suddenly switch to salty pizza as quickly as a bright, blue, *zig-zag* bolt of Uranian electricity. Aisha, she is the most beautiful girl. At the very least, she is interesting-looking. Her manner of dressing can stop you dead in your tracks. She is one of them who could grace the cover of a fashion magazine. She can wear some outfits a gypsy would envy, and her naked individuality can produce some mighty unique combinations. She'll usually be the first to wear a new fad, no matter how zany it is, yet she can also stick to Grandma's styles-even great-grandma's styles. With typical - Aquarian indifference.

She is a daring type who could just do thing differently from other people in her same society. She dares to fight for what she thinks belonged to her. Even when she acts confident, she mostly feels lonely and alone. If she fights with someone, she won't show any emotion even deep down inside pain and agony. Not for long she will come back to being the cheery and merry person again, because she looks at the world positively and has Faith in the word Love. She has more men friends than women friends, so do not be a jealous type if you date her. She could be slightly jealous, but she hates jealous guys. She loves Freedom so before and after marriage, her freedom has to be the same (though she is against marriage). She likes you to trust her, even if she does not trust you anyhow. She likes to be the one who is Right, so if you argue with her, let her win if it is not a big deal for you in that subject. She is a straight forward type, so if she does not like you anymore, she will just tell you straight to your face. Her love and relationship are always real, so if she says "It's over" be prepared to leave, she is not testing you. She is not a vulnerable type, so do not have to worry about her, she will survive by herself.

If she is with you when you get sick, she will certainly take care and look after you, even look after you mean "small loan". Do not have secret with her, she hates it and really can piss her badly. When she is sad, be understanding. When she is happy, be happy with her, she likes that. You will not get bored with Aisha. Someone who is close to her will know that deep down beneath that confident and cold-hearted person, she is just as fragile as any woman. She is a fun and talkative person and she likes to tease you. Do not let her talk alone, if you do, she will leave. She can float through her days and nights with all the grace of a proud swan, but she may behave like a clumsy bear in romantic situations (we had m ny and she escaped everytime). She says "There are so many miracles in the world for eyes to behold, it seems to her a terrible waste for two pairs of them to do nothing but gaze into each other's depths" (that ridiculous for her). She will be glad to let you take her and walk beside her as she looks with happy delight on the sunrise, an antique car, the milkman's horse, a yellow garbage pail, a stuffed owl or a red balloon caught in a church steeple. But don't distract her with too much to-get-her-ness. She has many type of jobs because she beliefs what a man can do, I can do. If you want her to work for you, forget it. When she is in love, (I feel) she will just leave her job in the day time just to come to see you, but not for long she will go back to work seriously again. Prepare to live and love with a "Working Woman" then you will be Ok. If she is mad, find a shelter for the "Hurricane" is here! Her bad temper will last very shortly though. She is not a revenge type and will not think of payback time. Most people might think of her as "One of a guy", but in fact she is a hundred percent woman. She is easily hurt, so be nice with her. If she really loves you, then you are lucky because she is an honest, truthful and will never bore you. Understand that sometimes she will be over confident and sometimes like to have power or act bossy. The quickest ways to lose her are to show jealousy, possessiveness or prejudice; to be critical, stuffy or ultra-conservative. You'll also have to like her friends, who will come in odd, assorted sizes and shapes.

She's susceptible to sudden flashes of inspiration, and her intuition is remarkable. Her judgment may not seem sound or practical at first, because she sees months and years ahead. She lives in tomorrow, and you can only visit there through her but enjoy her today to her fullest and will never even give you a hit what is there in her head about tomorrow and will live like there is no tomorrow. She's magic!!!

One day I was returning home from office so I decided to meet her and tell her that I was in love with her but doesn't know whether she likes me too or not. I called her up and asked her out for coffee but I became very sad because she was busy with her friends as she was leaving for a trip for a day with her parent's the day after and she denied meeting me and I felt gloomy.

I reached home after a while and I was watching television with my phone in my hand and was waiting for Aisha's reply but it never came. I texted her and asked her *text me whenever you get free*!

But that never came and I was losing my patience then my Dad came from office and my mother was sitting in a couch near me and my dad came and sat beside me and said

"You have to take a leave for seven days"— He sounded cold.

"For what seven days? It is very long" — I protested (not knowing the issue)

"We are going on a trip with the Rotary Club members" — he replied.

"I am not going with that boring group. Please dad you both go I will stay at home and I will enjoy more" — I argued.

"I didn't ask you, I am telling you. — He said. "And I don't want any discussions regarding this. You are coming and that's final"— He added.

"You are going" — He bellowed and I kept quiet and he left the room.

I didn't want to go because I wanted to be with Aisha and be alone with her when she returns from her trip and I could spend quality time with her and tell her that how much he loved her. But this wasn't happening my dad is pretty cool with me and as a friend but today he was different and I cannot do anything except to be quiet. We were going to Puri, Orissa after five days and I wasn't excited at all because I will not be meeting Aisha for long.

It was 14th August, the day arrived when we were leaving for Puri and there was no news from Aisha. She must be busy with herself and her exiting places. I reached the Gwalior railway station with my mother as my dad had already reached there with the other members and they were waiting for us on Platform No. 1. At the platform, a large number of passengers are waiting for the train. Some of them are sitting on the benches. Others are sitting on the bare ground or on their own boxes or trunks. Some are going up and down the platform. Every now and then they look in the direction from which the train is to come. When the distance single light is yellow, all feel happy. They are now certain that the train must come in short time. As soon as they catch sight of the smoke rising from the engine, they get ready and stand up. Some passengers carry their bundles on their heads, while others hold them under their arm pits. Some, whose luggage is too heavy to be carried by them, engage coolies for this purpose.

Our train was "Utkal Express which was to arrive at 4:05 pm but it got late and now it will arrive at 4:35 pm and I was looking for Ajit. Ajit is a friend as we both are from the same organisation and our parents are in the same club so we met and were friends. I was looking out for him with a heavy backpack on my back and then I saw a fair guy a cute, manly face (no female features). With a strong forehead. Thin to medium neckline, masculine. Nice muscle (manlike shoulders). His body type was average but in shape. Smart, confident, successful (because of his dad) educated (because he is smart). Sexy eyes that smile. Dark hair those were straight. Wearing a pink polo T-shirt and a pair of black jeans (I hate men wearing pink, though I never liked him he was always after the girls and really flirtatious. Whom I was saying I was the same but he was more than me). Here comes Ajit with his brown eyes towards me.

"OhhhyeahhhhhhVarunnnnnn! We are all set for Puri" — Ajit said with his regular exaggerating version. He always exaggerates his every word he says.

"Yeah" — I replied and gave a smirk. (I wasn't excited at all). "You seem very excited for the boring trip"— I replied as I added some sarcasm.

"Yessss Duddddeeee. It has been years I haven't been for a trip. I really needed a break and that too with a hot chick!!!!!" — he winked at me and whispered in my ears.

"Hot chick"?????" — I almost shouted (thank god mom wasn't there standing with me she moved to the ladies group where all the aunties were chatting together). I wasn't interested about the hot chick but in our club there was no girl of our age some were didi's and the other were kids and some were recently married but no girl of our age. He was always a player. He pointed out the girl and showed me a girl who was in Green.

A prison break, release, my feelings were at large.

What to do I asked myself, if only she would reciprocate my affection,

With ruffled complexion, I'm tortured by my minds misdirection,

Neuronal circuits put it to the vote but there is no election.

To divide and to section, to solve with mechanical perfection,

That's what my mind strives for; it's built to relentlessly question

The mystery prevails, can she and will she cure this infection?

I felt I was suffering from a disease and after all I can see my cure for it. So I was dreaming or a illusion every time. The crowd got gathered and there were thirty-three people who were coming with us and I was moving from my place and checking my eyes and confirming what I was looking at. And Ajit was blabbering continuously which was causing irritation.

Like an exotic flower she's an outstanding example, One of A kind,

She possess the qualities that gives pleasures to the senses,

A natural beauty without synthetic pretenses,

A heart of gold which gives value to the human,

A spirit that does not see herself as better than,

She possesses dignity and grace,

A woman who knows her rightful place,

She is at one with me, myself and I,

Not one to place herself on high,

She has no need to place others under her feet,

She's humbled, quiet and meek,

Her words are like music for me to hear,

And she's loved and everyone's dear.

How wonderful it is too see beauty characterised by dignity and grace,

Always greeting all she meets with a smile on her face,

Glamorous by the beauty by her magic potions,

She knows there is no such thing as a beauty lotion.

Her true beauty comes from within and it radiates through the natural glow of her skin.

Radiance is the quality of being bright and sending out rays of sunlight with a smile.

Her true beauty lets us know the quality of her being and her memory will outlast longer than a mere while.

The girl in green is Aisha who is only and only mine.

My heart skipped a beat like never before

And I was numb and wasn't sure what I saw.

"AISHAAA"???????? I almost SHOUTED! (Questions and exclamation marks over my head) — looking at her and not even blinked.

"You know her dude"!!!— looking straight into my eyes he said.

"No..No… neahhhhh! I don't know her I stammered. She is my neighbour so I have seen her" — I explained (but I didn't know why did I lied to him). I didn't know she is a club member too. (and this moment I was very thankful to dad for taking me to this trip or he knew about me and Aisha as because I have shared of me liking her, I didn't know I was confused but I wanted to hug my dad right now. seven days I and Aisha together and I am gonna tell her how much love I do have for her and propose her in this trip).

"You know she is a snob. Just before you came my mother was talking to her mother and she was standing beside so I said a Hi. She was doing something on her phone and she looked at me and got back to her phone without responding like I never exist" — what attitude man"— Ajit said angrily. (Because girls always die talking to her and this was the first to him… ha ha ha)

I was about to laugh out loud but then I controlled and said "Really"? "Must be a snob then" — I added but I wanted to laugh and I did not.

"But Brooooooo. She will talk to me. I challenge" — he replied boldly and I raised my eyebrow and wanted to kick his ass and drop him on the railway tracks and wanted him to say bloody as shole she's mine. Dare you look at her even but I remain quiet and wanted to see how rudely Aisha treats him. (*wink *wink)

May I have your attention please Train No. 12456 which is coming from Jammu Tavi and going to Puri is arriving on Platform No. 1 in some time — The Announcement.

The Train came and we had our tickets booked in coach A-2. There were so many people and so many bags. Aisha boarded the train without looking here and there. We were two young guys only so we were helping the coolies to put them under the birth inside the train which was truly tiring. I and Ajit got down from train to have some tea from the nearby tea stalls. We were sipping our tea and then….

"You insane, moron. What are you doing here" — someone shouted (I knew who was it but wasn't sure. I think you are thinking the same? Aren't you?)

Yep it was Aisha calling me (yep she has started to call me moron and stuffs told you she is a dude and an exotic flower) standing at the door of the train.

I smiled at her and the train blew the horn. Squealing of train brakes. I and Ajit threw the disposal cups and boarded the train and intricate Aisha to move but didn't say a word.

"Where are you going"??? She was gazing me out of excitement.

"Where is this train going Aisha"?? I added a little sarcasm and said.

"Puri!!!!" — She was blank.

"So I am also going to Puri" — I said.

"Oh god. You are" : she gave her the sweet pure smile that was just for me.

"But what are you doing here? You were going on a holiday in next week" — I questioned and asked her to get inside.

"Varun it is the next week" — She shrugged her shoulders and said.

"I thought you have gone because you never pinged me" — I protested (and had anger in me which I wanted to show but I hid it in).

"Why should I ping you every time, you are not my boyfriend"!! — she was blunt and gave me that which hurt me inside and my heart sank and out of all this Ajit was wondering actually what was happening.

As we pushed the door to get into the coach, a gentleman with a sophisticated look who had less hair and bald at the centre. He was wearing a yellow T-shirt with a pair of blue jeans. (I think I havc seen this man before). Ok he is the same man whom Aisha was holding his arms.

"Baba... Come inside" — the gentleman said to Aisha.

"And you Varun and Ajit come inside"— he said (He knows me how? Must know my dad). "You kids take a different compartment so no people will disturb you and you guys can have all fun" — He winked at us and went (OMG such a cool dad I was wondering that my dad is the coolest one no I was wrong and the gentleman is Aisha's dad, hope you get that *wink*)

We took four births 13,14,15,16 as Aisha wanted because it was far from the parents.

"But we are just three and the 4th one will be occupied by some elder for sure" — Ajit made it a point this time and he was standing on his way.

"No-one will occupy that one" — Aisha snapped. "Because my friend is coming" — She added.

Aisha always gives me traumas, now my head was spinning thinking what kind of friend will it be. Whether a he-friend or a she-friend. If she-friend comes then its fine and if he-friend comes.......

"AAAAAiiiiiiiiiiiiiissssssssssssssssssssshhhhhhhhhhhhhhhhhh" - Someone shouted so loud that the full train got a thump of her voice.

It was a girl who was average looking with a tan skin and was fat (not fat but just with a heavy built and looks stronger that will be good I hate girls calling fat). She was wearing a white top with big pink, orange and purple flowers printed on them like she was going to Hawaii and wearing a pair of green jeans (I wonder how can anyone can wear green denims, anyways it her wish but personally I didn't like it) but this made me happy that a little-on-muscle girl was her she-friend for sure and this made me relaxed.

"Ishitaaa! Thank god you are here, I was about to call you else you would have missed the train again" — Aisha exclaimed. (Means she had missed her train a lot of times, I can smell that and you? And I knew her name is Ishita like you all:)

Aisha took the window I mean near the window and got settled on the lower birth and the Ishita sat next to Aisha and near the aisle and I and Ajit took the opposite birth and I took the window and Ajit the aisle but was staring diagonally and I hated that. Aisha introduced her friend to both of us and she still behaved that Ajit didn't exist but Ishita behaved like she knows all of us from childhood and which was great to Ajit.

"And you said you didn't know Aisha"!!! — Ajit whispered to my ears and eyed at me.

"She is my neighbour I told you before" — I whispered back again. Yes anyone would die to be near Aisha. She is everyone's dream and everyone's heart throb. She is the one !!! All of a sudden the girls started giggling. They just need it! Giggling every time.

It was 11:00 pm after a lot of chit chatting and gossiping and listening to songs and Ajit hitting on Aisha and Ishita hitting on me, we took our respective births to sleep after having a heavy dinner. Aisha took the upper birth and Ishita the lower one in the vertical direction. Ajit fought with me and took the upper birth just to be with Aisha but I know who was Aisha Roy : She plugged her earphones into her ears and went off to sleep and didn't even look at him. (Ha Ha Ha I was loving it). Our parents also were asleep and Ishita was struggling with her bag and was searching sc mething in it and looking at me and smiling. I took the pillow and looked outside but nothing was visible because of darkness and then to Aisha as I could see her because she was diagonal to me. But she was asleep and then I closed my eyes and fell asleep. I couldn't sleep but I had to shut my eyes all because of the new person Ishita.

"You slept you Moron, Dumbo!! Get up idiot!" — Ishita was shouting I guess and pushing my arm I couldn't make ›ut who was it as I was dead asleep.

No I was dreaming! — I again went back to sleep. Someone kicked me.

Aisha was standing in front of me with the night lamp on. Ishita was sitting on the birth like the way before I went off to sleep still struggling with her brown handbag and Ajit was peeping from the upper birth.

"You guys don't know how to have fun" — Aisha commented.

"Who said? Boys can have all the fun" — He said with a flirtatious tone.

"SHUT UP"— said Aisha. She snapped rudely very rude. And on the contradictory Ajit was quiet and I controlled my laugh in my pillow and covered my sheet.

"Varun quick go and check it out if everyone is asleep" — Aisha ordered.

I sneaked and checked everyone and all were asleep I reported Aisha.

"But what is the scene"? — I asked. I was very curious to know (whether we were making out or what. LOL)

"This" — Ishita said. As she took out a huge one litre bottle of Blenders Pride whiskey.

And our eyes and tongues were out like when a dog sees a bone that is ready to grab it. Ajit eyes were glittering and so were mine.

"By the way we girls don't giggle unnecessarily. Let me tell you that— said Ishita. She looked at me and winked and I quickly snatched my gaze from her.

I was making the drink for all in the disposal glasses (which were strong and of different colours. Girls are so creative) because Miss Aisha doesn't like to make a drink and have (her drinking attitude). With all varieties of chips, peanuts and cashew and then we all sat together and said "Cheers"!

Aisha was having fun with three of us. Yes three because she behaved like Ajit never exist. Man how does she does that. She is so arrogant but I love her arrogance for strangers and love for her friends like me and Ishita. (Yes like friends only till now). And with a Pure heart. And the gossip starts its fun to be around girls when they laugh on silly things and ask you to open the bottle when it is difficult for them. After three pegs Ishita was completely high and she hugged me and now was sitting right next to me on my right and Ajit was on my left because Aisha didn't allow him to sit near her. I could make out that Aisha was sad after drinking. That day too after the party she was crying on the terrace and today also. What's their inside her and when we know each other now. Why can't she just share her stuff with me? What is it? Her life? Her parents are cool. What else it can be. Is it her work? (no work cannot make Aisha cry). What is it??

"Chal let's play some game" — Aisha said suddenly.

"Yeahhhhh let's play kiss your crush game"— Ishita said like three sheets to the wind.

I could figure out a shadow coming and I thought about the co-passengers as I was drunk. She was a woman. She looks wonderful in a green colour saree that set off her skin tones. She wore it in an elegant way, where the complementary tones of skin and the cloth make her look wonderful. Aisha was sitting on Ishita's birth alone holding her disposal glass filled with whiskey and then I realised the wonderful looking woman was Aisha's mother. I gazed at Ajit but he doesn't know her and I squeak and my voice chocked almost when I whispered to Ajit's ears that she is Aisha's mother and the same happened with Ajit. I was sitting the same way Ishita to my right and Ajit to my left.

"Kids! You guys are still awake" — Aisha's mother stood in front of us and looking at us. "It is 4:30 am"!— she added.

We all went in shock (except Ishita) because wasn't in her own sense. We were caught red-handed with the filled glasses of whiskey that too in front of our friend's mother. Now this parent will go on and tell every parent and my head was wobbling when Aisha said,

"Mom, Come sit here" — Aisha patted on the birth.

Both of our mouths were open like someone kicked in our teeth. Aisha is calling her mother to sit with her when she has a full whiskey glass in her hand and also in ours. "And what happened to her"? — Aisha's mom asked pointing out at Ishita.

"Ha ha nothing just the emotional trigger for Varun because of the alcohol" — Aisha replied her mom. Where we both were numb and was just gazing what was happening actually. God her mom knew that her daughter drinks. God she is the coolest mother on earth I must say Hats off!! I am actually amazed and shivering at the same time I haven't seen anyone like her parents the coolest on earth.

"Kids go off to sleep and talk low else anyone would get up and could catch you drinking" — She was making us aware. (***APPLAUSE***) ha haha!! This was amazing. She was making us aware. She was a friend to us. But I and Ajit were shocked to see Aisha so comfortable with her mom and we both were like we had killed someone and we had a knife in our hands with blood drops on the knife and the dead body was lying in front of us. But it was like the knife was artificial and so was everything. She was the super Aunt. Aisha had a big sip from her glass and her mom said to take it slow. She wished us good night and she left.

"God your mother is so cool. WOW. That's incredible" — I said.

"Are you sure she won't tell it to the other parents" — Ajit asked quickly.

"Don't worry *beta*, I won't."— She removed the curtain and said and left. And we all were numb and we put Ishita to her birth and made her sleep and when we went back to sleep it was 5:15 in the morning.

It was 4:46. I looked at my watch and was wondering was it morning or afternoon, I couldn't make out then I removed the curtain from the window and saw the sun out and then realised it was 4:47 pm and we were still sleeping. I rubbed my eyes and saw Ajit and Ishita sitting in front of me on Ishita's birth and some stranger was sitting on the side birth with completely grey hair who was wearing thick spectacles and was watching Ajit and Ishita with round eyes and with great interest of what they were doing as they were talking and whispering in a low tone (flirtatious) and then I looked up for Aisha who was still sleeping on her upper birth which was diagonal to me. I was lying on bed straight and Ishita gave me a smile and Ajit a normal look.

Baba! Baba! — Aisha's dad came to call Aisha. (Both of them call baba to each other).

"Baba!Babai"!!— Her dad was calling her by different names and pampering her like a new born baby. "Baba get up you haven't had anything since 15-16 hours. Get up baba, see all your friends are up" — Aisha dad said trying to wake her up.

"Babbbaaa...ahaaanahaan" — Aisha moaned sweetly like a new born baby as well. "Baba pleaseeee" — She moaned and replied. (Omg what tantrums my parents never wake me up like this or I haven't seen anyone and father counting she haven't had anything, that is so sweet). He pulled up her bed sheet up from her face and she pulled up again and covered the face and went off to sleep again.

"Aisha get up"— Ishita said (As her dad ask her to do so).

"Ishita. Shut up" — Aisha snapped rudely.

"Baba get up, get up and pulled her hand and made her sit on the birth and said it is chicken for lunch" — His said.

But Aisha was wearing on the upper birth with bed sheets wrapping all around her and her pillow made her a new hairstyle and she looked like a cute little angel and a cute lovely baby. Managing to open her eyes she said "what baba-chicken?"

Yes chicken is her favourite though she have's it every day without Mondays and she is having it from the time she learnt to eat. Yes I do wonder too how one cannot get bored of having chicken every day. But she is Aisha. (Till now you must have known how she is). She quickly came down and we all had our lunch and we finished having when it was 5:20 pm and Ajit and Ishita ended up having their paneer-butter masala which I tasted but Aisha didn't because she hates paneer.

11:00 pm we were all sitting together and this was the second night in the train and we all were listening to different songs sometimes asking Ishita to sing because she's a lovely singer and throughout the day I thought of the incident last night that if Aisha's mother tell my parents what will happen and I am checking their moods and everything was normal and I and Ajit was struggling to have a fag in the train in the washrooms as it is not allowed. And here Ajit was still trying on Aisha but Aisha behaved the same.

"Hey Guys good night, I am going off to sleep"— announced Aisha.

"Why Aisha? Why so early??"— said Ishita. "Yeah let's talk"— I added and Ajit just came a please look.

"Because I am sleepy. As simple as that" — said Aisha.

"Oh yeah Miss Beauty queen needs her full beauty sleep" — Ishita said and winked at her. She smiled and Aisha went off to sleep. Ajit laughed a little late and Aisha responded like no one was there. I don't know how she manages to do that. Incredible!

It was 5:30 am and we reached Puri, everyone was ready with their luggage's except Aisha I tried hard to wake her up but she is she and then his father came and woke her up and she was asleep but though standing and his dad asked her not to touch her bag because it was heavy and it might cause pain later. (What pamperness). I think she has got everything. Whatever she touches she gets it. I should say she is a lucky girl and anyone who will get all her love will leave his everything just because of her. She is a heart bless. She is a rare flower.

After the view of the sea from the car while coming from the station. We reached our hotel "Hotel Victoria". This three-star rooms, with bath, has a functional layout and quiet location with views of the sea and the beach was magnificent. I could see all the people having fun on the beach but small in size because we were on the 6th floor and the view was staggering. Light, modern and functional. The three-star rooms offer twin beds and every comfort. The bathroom has a shower, bath and toilet as standard. There is also a television, telephone and safe.

"Hey, you idiot. You are still not ready". She came into my room like a superfast express train. Though she wasn't ready yet. (Getting ready as in-getting ready for the beach. Yes she is gonna go inside the sea)

"Ready? Ready for what"— I acted like I didn't know. Ajit was sitting on one of the beds and staring at Aisha. She came close to me and said we need alcohol.

"But Aisha it is just 9:00 a.m. and you want to booze'? — I exclaimed (because I was getting possessive and started to care for Aisha and I don't want her to booze every time because this will affect her health).

"Ok then do one thing, (Ishita entered but then she looked at her and again continued). When will go to the beach with our parents and when after getting wet in the sea you may feel for booze then they will ask you where are you going *beta*. Then you reply *"THEKE PE"* — she shouted.

I, Ajit and Ishita laughed out loud like insane people.

"Ok ok hold on Miss Aisha Roy. Even if we get the booze how we will drink in front of our parents" — I teased.

"Oh hello Mr. Manager; (She always calls me with different names) she said sarcastically. Come (she showed me a man selling coconut water from the balcony). Did you get it or I have to exaggerate?? Ajit and Ishita said — What is happening?

"We will mix the alcohol in the coconut water dumbo. Hope you got it now" — She teased me back.

"But where we will find an alcohol shop here"— enquired Ajit. "Yeah from where we will get"— I added. She sat on the bed where Ishita was sitting and said as soon as you get down go out of the hotel and turn right there is a liquor shop. — She said in a relaxed way.

'But how do you know Aishhhhh- Ishita said. We never crossed over hotel. So how do you know there is a shop"— Ishita enquired.

"Yes how do you"— Exclaimed I and Ajit together.

"Guys this is my ninth time to Puri. So go ahead and go change and mix the vodka in the coconut water and stay there near the coconut seller. I and Ishita will reach in a while" — she said and went with Ishita back to her room which was just next to ours.

We were on the beach, the sunlight glittering on every grain of sand, the beach idyllic, white and fresh. This beach has few people resting on its pillow like, floor. The sea washes in; a small wave washes across the sand dissolving the remaining foot prints of its inhabitants. The beach is in a cove, a tranquil, iridescent, perfect cove the sail boats, so elegant in design dock at a local harbour, I watch from my view point on the white sandy beach, as the captains of each ship slowly step on to dry land like aliens landing on a strange planet. My worries disappear as the crystal water touches my toes, its warm soft touch echoes through my body. The tide so slow and delicate in swallowing the sand beneath my feet, I hardly notice the small fish in this glass like water edging further and further towards. I was wearing a brown 3/4th with a move T-shirt and Ajit was wearing blue shorts with a white t-shirt. We were on vacation and everyone was happy and I was happy because Aisha is with me and I am going to tell her about my feelings for her. I was happy and excited but nervous. Aisha came down escorting Ishita. Aisha was wearing an orange sun dress which had two strips and her back was bare and her front too but her cleavage wasn't visible at all she was very particular about herself she never wanted her to be seen by everyone only the things which she feels that's it is only skin. The dress was too short and too above her knees and she was wearing a large round cream colour hat because she doesn't want the sun to hit her eyes. Ishita was wearing a black tight 3/4th and a loose pink t-shirt. So her extra curves aren't visible. I gave Aisha the Vodka-coconut water and I and Ajit shared from one. After sipping up the whole vodka I think Aisha had most of it. And she asked all of us to get inside the water but Ishita was scared of water so she never went. Ajit was showing some thrilling activities to impress Aisha but he banged his right leg with a huge stone and she asked me to come I denied because I don't like water not that I am very scared of water but not that friendly even. She changed herself into hot denims and a blue ganji and was wearing the awesome looking glares which made her look marvelous. Ajit who bumped his leg was sitting on the rest chair and staring at Aisha and I wanting to snatch his eyes and I eyed him for stop staring at her and then she continued with Ishita who was sitting right next to him. We all were under the huge colourful umbrella and was chit-chatting, Ishita was playing with the sand and we all were clicking pictures of ours and Aisha and our parents who just joined us. I was looking at Aisha who was splashing in the water alone, playing sometimes with her dad and most of the time alone and I was still sipping my vodka coconut water and suddenly I could look for Aisha. She wasn't in the same place. Her dad was there but she wasn't there. I removed my glares and my eyes were searching for her. I asked the two whether they could see our friend Aisha but she wasn't visible then after a while Ishita said "God! Look, there she is". She was in the middle of the sea and that too all alone. Ishita was smiling but I was frightened. I was waving by hands to her, we all were but she was alone with the waves in a tube, she was all on her own. I searched for her dad and I stood beside him near the shore and asked.

"Uncle! Let's call the lifeguard she is so far" — I said in trepidation.

"Ha haha!! Lifeguard? Oh no no— she is enjoying herself and the lifeguard is there to guard her. Don't worry she will come back"— Her dad said but was waiting for her daughter.

After thirty minutes Aisha came and we all were waiting, actually I was waiting because I was angry as I was very worried for her. She came up with a big smile to us and said "it was Heaven inside. It was amazing like a wonderland. You guys should have come in it would be fun" and sat near the rest chair on my left and wiping herself with a towel.

"Why you had to go in the middle of the sea? I know you are a fun loving girl and I know what you want you get but why this type of activities" — I almost shouted.

"Why means what Mr. Varun Mall??? It is my life! My wish. I will do whatever I feel like which makes me happy."— She snapped

"I was concerned if something would have happened to you"— I explained and showing my wordiness.

"Listen Varun I am not afraid of dying. I wish I would have died pretty earlier and I would leave the earth happily"— She shouted and snapped at me. And I kept quiet and so did Ishita and Ajit.

"And I DON'T get everything I want Mr. Varun"— she warned.

She grabbed her things and put it in her bag and asked Ishita to come with her and she went along with her. She turned and said "Varun you don't know anything about my life"!!!! And she left.

I stood there totally numb I wanted to say something to calm her, I couldn't think of anything because my head was wobbling with words of Aisha of "I wish I would have died earlier", "you don't know anything about my life". What is it? What is in my life that I don't know? I thought I know her quite well. I thought she has nothing to hide from me. But I was wrong. What's the thing? Is she depressed on something? I thought she has a perfect life. I have known her for three months now but never seen this phase of her. I wanna know!!!!!

It was 8:18 pm I looked my watch and I and Ajit was getting ready for the party which was to be held in the banquet hall which was organised by the club members. No glimpse of Aisha, Ishita came to our room a lot of times after the scene on the beach but Aisha wasn't in sight. I and Ajit reached the banquet hall. I was wearing a camel colour pant and a black polo t-shirt. While Ajit was wearing a pair of blue jeans and a green T-shirt. Ishita was dancing on the floor with the elderly aunties and uncles wearing a turquoise blue top and yellow legging which was looking pretty good. (I loved the colours). But my eyes didn't stick there I was searching for Aisha, My Aisha. And then my eyes froze at a corner where She was sitting wearing a while frill dress which had frills all over and she looked like a real angel. She was sitting alone and looking everybody on the dance floor. "But I didn't know angels fly so low". The phrase completely fits here. I went near Aisha and Ajit got busy dancing with the elderly people and I whispered 'Sorry' into Aisha's ears and she didn't respond and reacted the same way like I never exist. Ishita came to Aisha and for the same reason obvious (she was hitting on me dude) and I called Ajit and we four asked if they were enjoying Aisha gave me a strong look and didn't responded. I asked them if they were having fun, I don't know about others but certainly Aisha wasn't enjoying at all. So I made a plan and told them lets all get to the beach and drink there as I already took a full Whiskey bottle "Teachers" and asked them about the plan. Everyone accepted including Aisha. We headed towards the beach and the, enclosed, beach is silent. The bright ball blinds you as it emerges; it rises like a yellow lollipop on the distant horizon. Crashing against the shore, small waves wash the night's debris onto the land. Untouched golden sand covers the floor as far as your eyes can see. Soothing, a gentle sea breeze rustles through your hair. Beach shops prepare for their day of excited costumers bustling in and out of their small seafront shops. Opening their doors, they bring out their entire beach products looking out to the sea you can see the large cruise ships on the world's edge. We took a place and sat on the sand in a group. I made the drink and made the first drink and gave to Aisha and said sorry again. She took the glass and said Ok but didn't smile. I just want her to smile I want her smile nothing else. We all drank in a hurry and we all were pretty high because we were down with four pegs and we were discussing life, love, philosophy etc.

"What do you think about love"? "What's your statement? — asked Ishita to all.

"Oh babe! Love is getting one after the other" — Said Ajit.

"Shut up Ajit. Being in love is such a wonderful feeling. That one person who dies caring for a girl, he's the person who makes her feel she is the only girl on this planet earth" — described Ishita. (Aisha was silent she didn't say a word and I wanted her to participate because I wanna know whether she is single even or not).

"What do you think Varun"??— asked Ishita and Ajit.

"Ummm Love .... Ajit as you know I was not the love kind of a person. And I never thought I will ever fall in love but I don't know about the future. Yeah but for me if you seek to be loved you may be disappointed because you cannot control others, you cannot ask for love because it is not a favour it is a GIFT!!!!!!" — I replied.

"True it is a GIFT and not all receive that. And do you really believe that"? — exclaimed Aisha to me.

"Yeah I do"— I replied and continued.

"But if you seek to be loved,

If you seek to become the gift,

You will succeed,

So become the pillar of light,

A fountain of love,

A source of comfort!"

"I totally agree with Varun"— said Ishita.

"And even if you cannot help, the mere act of loving lightened their burdens, for they find consolation in your concern. When you follow this path, the love you willingly give will be returned to you, you will be loved without seeking it." — I said

"Ha haha. Varun you really seem so (I can sense some sarcasm in her laugh). If you love a person, the person will love you back"? "Have you ever loved anyone?— What a crap is this? Fucking irritating" — said Aisha in an irritably tone.

"You know what—Love is shitty, Love is devastating, Love is a total waste of time and there is nothing called love, people just use one another. Some are used one-sided and ended up with a heartbreak that's it" — announced Aisha.

"Aisssssshhhhhh. Why are you saying this? I am shocked to hear, Aisha you are the one who used to say Love does exist and all the sweet words and gifts of love." — said Ishita astonished

"There is nothing called Love, I was wrong I was a fool" — she said and had the half-filled whiskey from her glass and threw it on the sand.

"Have you guys ever fallen in love? Do you know even what love is"? — Aisha said (she was legless, she was completely drunk and there I can see tears in her eyes but it was inside it had not fallen out). She sat on the sand with her legs folded like a little obedient girl and wearing the white frill dress making her look like a pearl and her dress the shell.

"I had many crushes and I have been with many girls but not love—I think six months was the highest" — explained Ajit.

"That is not love dude" — drunken Aisha said.

"You and you"??— Aisha was standing and drooling and pointed out to Ishita and me asked about our thoughts.

"Never fallen before......" I didn't complete but Aisha took the conversation from me and started.

"Ahhhh....... I will tell you a story of Love. You wanna hear it? —Drunk Aisha said and searching a place to sit in the same position where she was already sitting. Now, here it goes..........

21st December 2010, I sent a friend request on Facebook, I saw him after seventeen years and we were friends when I was of four and he was eight. He has grown up now and didn't know whether he will recognise even or not but still I sent. And that time I was in Delhi doing my graduation and we used to get very less time checking Facebook and stuff. After some days when I checked it again there was no respond to my friend request. 1st Jan 2011. A message in my Facebook inbox popped up. The message was.

*I cannot believe my eyes, that I am talking the small sweet Winnie who used to play with me when we were kids. You look the same but only prettier. I hope you remember our childhood times. I think this year will be a great one! Give my regards to uncle and aunty and wish them Happy New Year from my side.

Cheers

Arpan.*

"That's so sweeeeeeeeeeeeeeeeeeeeeeeet"— exclaimed Ishita.

I replied to him was...

hey, I am good. Yeah, it has been seventeen years and I don't remember our good times but I think they were wonderful and thank you for the wishes and wish the same to you

He replied—

Oh, I regret that your memory restricts and you don't remember me as kid. Let me tell you this that you were very fond of me as a kid. I still remember you have "wetty palms". You are still the same?

11th January 2011, another facebook message popped up from Arpan "I am not very active on facebook let's get catch up on phone my #number is-09971111195

13th January 2011 a text in my phone was received it was from Arpan. The message says

** Shall I call you Aisha or Winnie? **

I replied— **anything you like**

He replied ** Ok then I will call you Madhuri Dixit from now. Ha! Ha!**

I replied ** Aisha will be good**.

I had come to Gwalior for my vacation and was with my family and having a good time and I was returning to Delhi after my Holi holidays. And Arpan was in Delhi working there in a private firm. After a lot of texts and messages and then we met after two months; after birthday and Valentine's Day wishes we met !

26th March 2011, Venue: Select Citywalk. We both decided the venue and we decided the time at 10:00 am sharp. I reached by 9:30 am sharp at the decided venue and I reached before because I am very punctual about my time. I was living in Saket and the Mall was few minutes away so I had to take an auto-rickshaw so I reach early. Costa-Coffee was the place where I sat and started to wait for him and called Arpan and asked him that he had left for the Mall or not and he replied yes and he said he will be there in half an hour. This happened for another three hours where I was waiting and at costa-Coffee and he was coming in half an hour. It was 1:30 pm and then after a lot of hide and seek he was there in the parking area and I was fucking angry but controlled and waited for him but we didn't decided where to meet and we had a deal that we will search for each other and not meet like the other people. After disconnecting the phone and quickly touch up my gloss and my hair and went on searching for Arpan my Childhood friend who was searching for me as well and I was excited and nervous because this was my first date. Arpan called me and said "Hey where are you"? "Ok now you have waited for me for so long let me give you a hint". "BEAN"!!!

"coffee and bean na"— I replied. And he asked me to come out near the coffee and bean shop and he said he was standing out near the Verna car display. I went out and the sun was hitting my eyes and I hated it and he was still on the phone. I was wearing a blue colour dress with green and purple checks which was above my knee and my hair was till my shoulders black and straight. I reached outside the coffee and bean shop and was searching for him though I have seen his pictures on facebook I guess I can identify him but I was looking around near the car display but no glimpse of his. All the people was looking at me that what I was searching. I changed my way and moved the other side. I was still on the phone and Arpan said "STOP!! STOP!!"— Ahhh Blue dress! you look good "— Arpan said.

"Nice blue footwear"— he said and I stopped when I was walking. I was surprised I was looking here and there but couldn't find him and I was smiling yeah a smile and confused look was on my face.

"Ok now stop and walk five steps forward"— I started to walk and he counted and I stopped.

"Now look up"— he ordered. I looked up but couldn't find him. I looked up to the area where it was legal on the mall but he said to look more higher and then I could see a young man wearing a blue shirt and

Waving both his hands one was occupied by his phone and the other with flowers. That was the moment. My best moment in my life!! It was the best trust me the best feeling ever and my first date. Yes he was Arpan!!!

He came down and we hugged each other formally. He had a perfect body, heighted about 5'11 inches, rigged out with muscles like a ship with ropes, its limbs appearing to open out like a star around that fleece where there rises, in contrast to woman it has that amazing simile, "rigged out with muscles like a ship with ropes" which alone is worth an evening's awestruck contemplation, and the star, and the fleece. It may not be perfect, but it is still very, very good. Her flawless olive skin accentuated her pecan shaped hazel eyes. His voice was so warm and comforting even the stingiest of strangers immediately warmed up to him. He had substantial and fleshy lips. He gave me the flowers and said it matches with your dress because the flowers he gave it to me were blue orchids. My first flowers and My first Orchids. We were all blue in colour I he and the flowers :

"You are the same. Just bigger and prettier" — said Arpan with a smile.

"Thank you"— I blushed and became red and was excited and nervous as it was my first date of my life and my heart was thumping out to my ribs and was feeling nervous. We sat in cinnamon like an eating stop and then we went for a movie "red riding hood". And he stared at me many times and when I asked him why are you staring. So he said that — "I am trying to see that you are really so innocent or you are trying to show".

Days came and go and we got close day by day. Meeting him on weekends..it was like a fairy tale

I met the man in the meads;

Tall, glamorous with no beard

His hair was short, black and light

And his eyes were wild.

He said— he will make brooches and toys for my delight

Of bird sing at morning and star shine at night

He looked at me as he did love;

And made a sweet moan.

I fell in love with him but didn't know

Was he thinking of us thick as snow?

Second April 2011, We had planned on Friday itself that we would have a night out at India Gate, the most appropriate place for celebrations; If India won the World Cup. From the very first ball of the match we were glued to the TV set. We were a group of six people watching the match in 'Keya' in Promenade mall in Vasantkunj, New Delhi. We didn't get any tickets in the PVRs and all coz they were already running house full. So, we thought of staying indoors and admire the beauty of the game. It was a disputable toss. Nevertheless match started and India was on fire. Electric fielding and some terrific piece of bowling. We were enjoying every bit of it. Zaheer bowled a magical spell and also provided a breakthrough. We had estimated that Sri Lanka would be restricted to less than 240 runs but they went all the way to score 274. Now was the time for the most awaited Indian batting. And check this out!!! The second delivery of Malinga dismissed Sehwag and a shock ran thru our bodies. Sachin followed him after some time, falling to a rather loose ball off the same Malinga. The whole atmosphere was calm and cold. It appeared as some Tsunami had struck. Some replied that we could still do it and asked not to lose hope. Some said that they would also quit if another couple of wickets followed. I was busy with my two friends and Arpan and his two friends were also there who was watching the match.

After half an hour it appeared that we were getting stable. Now all the people in the room stuck to their myth. One friend didn't change his sitting position for the rest of the match. One was going to have a piss when a wicket fell so he controlled for the next 25 overs. He felt that since he had done it in the toilet a wicket had fallen. I didn't put my mobile down throughout the innings as I believed that something bad would happen if I did it. The wickets were falling when the cell was not in my hand. We all followed our superstitions until the final six was hammered by Dhoni. Now was our time. We WON!!!!!! Yes INDIA WON the World Cup 2011.

We started off. Arpan took his car and we all started off six of us fitting in a Maruti Alto. I took the front seat for the obvious reasons. On the way we encountered immense celebration and crazy fans. At some places we also got down to celebrate and clicked pictures, waved at the other commuters hooting and whistling. All reacted to everyone that day which is very unusual in Delhi where the people are so engrossed in themselves that they don't mind what the other person is doing. We were two kms away from India Gate when we all gave up. He said that if we walked we could make it faster. So, we thought of having a walk with the crowd by our side. The whole population was out on the roads shouting, bursting crackers, shouting slogans and hugging strangers. Proud fans in hundreds and thousands including women and children of all ages thronged India Gate to celebrate the victory after 28 years of wait. Youngsters hit the streets in cars and on motorcycles shouting "India, India". People were dancing on the bonnets of their cars. There were more people on the tops than inside the cars. Overall it was a mind blowing atmosphere something to die for. But something more happened that day.

Arpan came to me leaving (Pankaj and Aayush) whom he was walking with and I was walking with (Taina and Shivani). Suddenly Arpan came to me and said—

"I saw a lily on the bow

With anguish mist and fever dew;

Your cheeks are red as rose;

Why you did suddenly froze?

I will make garlands for you head;

And bracelets too, and piece of zone

This will be for us and none.

I will make the food,

And you shall keep in your room

Where white flows the river

And bright brows the broom.

I will be your music

When no one is near;

The fine song of singing,

The rare song to hear.

You are my roots who is immense sweet

With honey wild and manna dew,

And sure in language he said,

I Love you true...."

Yes, he proposed to me in front of everyone with a lot of excitement in my heart, my legs shivering, I had tears in my eyes with a wide smile. I nodded and said yes. The celebration became double and all our friends were happy about our well-being. I was truly happy but I was sad because day after tomorrow I was leaving Delhi after completing my graduation, and after living for four years in this city which made me nostalgic and I was, I was leaving Arpan which was the saddest part.

It was 4th April 2011, I was going back to Gwalior and I knew it would be extremely difficult to come down to Delhi just to meet Arpan. This time I wasn't going alone I will be with Arpan's memories. It was 5:47 am and I was standing on the platform all alone with my two heavy baggage and my backpack. (All my friends went home as I stayed back for a few more days just because of Arpan). The train arrived on time and I started to walk to my coach which was C-5 of Shatabdi Express. I was trolling my luggage and someone came and held my waist and I got panicked wondering who it was. A man wearing a green checks full sleeves shirt and a pair of blue jeans stood in front of me. I was frightened, surprised and shocked. My lips fell apart in disbelief. I was amazed and pulled the man's collars and kissed him on his lips on the platform like we were only their present. It seemed like a dream as what I was feeling came right in front of me. Yes it was Arpan. He came to see me off and wanted to see me the last time and said it were the best days of life. I took my seat and had some tears in my eyes of being departed from my love and checked my bag for a tissue and what I got was a book in my bag which was not bought by me it was wrapped and it was P.S. I love you. With a note inside which says— Your smile is everything to me —Love Arpan.

I was back to Gwalior and I was working in my own company and I cannot leave the business every time and visit Delhi every month, so it was really difficult to make it up to meet him. We used to meet once in two months. Some months were really good. While for some time we were able to meet for a sandwich or lunch and hangout downtown getting together with your love. We had a serious lack of face time, we had alternatives because we were in the modern era so we have phone calls, text messages video callings and other communication devices developed since the carrier pigeon.

It was going really well, we were meeting twice in a month and the long phone calls in the night and setting our own boundaries and not doing the things the partner doesn't like, we both did it until when one day at 3:00 am in the morning Arpan called me (he never calls me so late in the night) and said,

"Baby I want to say something to you"— He said (I could sense that something weird or unnatural was going to happened without any pause I asked him what is it).

"Simran, will be coming home tomorrow as it is our off day and she wants to spend some time with me, I denied her. But she invited herself and I couldn't deny her any more" — Arpan said and explained before I could say anything. Simran was Arpans colleague who were working with him for the last two years together and Simran used to like Arpan (what I was told). And so I used to hate that female and never wanted to hear her name but he did it and he made me sad. I replied by just saying Ok and kept down the phone. The next night Arpan was with Simran, he didn't call me. But I called him at 11:00 pm, 1:00 am and 2:00 am but the phone was unanswered and the next morning when he called me he said she was there with him till 4:00 am which made me sad but I didn't utter a word. I was hurt completely shattered but I didn't say anything because I didn't want to fight.

Distance may be fine for relatives and old friends, but when it comes to romantic love-that mysterious chemical reac ion that sets off when two people occupy the same physical space-the long distance relationship is a poor excuse for the real thing. Sometimes there is nothing more erotic than a disembodied voice, no question mark tantalising than a whispered "What are you wearing?" especially when you can make the answer. To believe in disembodied voice, to be as smitten with his absence as I am with his presence, is to be a true romantic. It was to love for your future, it was to believe in the impossible, or at least the improbable. After a year things were the same with me but not with him. He was a changed man now and he was every time busy with his work even at 1:00 am which was not believable to me because my instinct works like no one and I have a long list of friends who are residing every part of the world and a lot of times I have caught him when he was watching a movie with Simran and holding hands with her as my friends told me because they were in the same movie theatre but I never said a word and I didn't believe my friends eyes but I want to trust him because I loved him and will not doubt him but my instinct said I was wrong. And I felt he was lying to me and parting away from me but I was trying hard, sending him gifts and letters every month making phone calls and messages and asking about his health. But all the things were the same, no calls from him when I am ill and upset or when I am travelling. We were completing almost two years and it was my birthday again and he came down to Gwalior just to greet me and I was really Happy to see him and I felt I have got my Love back to my life. After a day well spent he went back to Delhi where he was living alone.

One day, it was 8th Feb 2013 and I felt something very weird going inside my heart, I felt restless and I opened Simran's profile on Facebook. I opened her profile picture and it was a shadow picture of a lean tall guy and a girl holding hands on a muddy path. By just looking at the picture I got it, it was Arpan. I was very sure. I was shivering, I was lost, I was sobbing and I was shocked. I dialed her number with my shivering fingers and called her up and asked her who was in her profile picture and she said it was just a internet picture which she liked it and put in. I replied her by saying that if anything was going between you two I will be out of your and his life but she denied and asked me to trust her but couldn't and I called Arpan and asked about the picture but he blasted on me and said stop doubting him and I was ashamed what I was thinking of what I was thinking about him. We hardly spoke to each other now. It was the last day of February and I was excited about Arpan's birthday which was on 3rd March and I texted him that I will come to Delhi on his birthday but he denied and he said he was going on a trip with his clients who was coming from USA to some hill station. I didn't tell him I had booked my tickets already and took permission from my parents knowing the fact that I and Arpan were in a relationship but they never objected and took any actions against us though they were sad and unhappy about me having a relationship with him.

Third March 2013, 8:00 am, I was at the Indira Gandhi International Airport, terminal-3 at New Delhi. I was going to Chennai with my dad for some business work. "Passengers boarding a flight to Goa are advised to check in at Gate 8. Fifteen minutes left for checking in. There is an announcement asking all the passengers to that flight to check in at Gate 22 with their boarding passes". Then there is this mad rush across the lounge where the young and strong make it easily jumping over the furniture, mothers with children become reckless, loose a child or some hand baggage, the old and the infirm almost loose all hope of boarding the flight in time. When they all check in finally there is the next announcement saying the flight is delayed by 30 minutes for 'technical reasons'. "While I sat in those blue chairs waiting for my flight boredom set in, though I contemplated flicking through the pages already twice read in the paper I had purchased from the small shop that sold wall to wall crossword books. My attention was caught by the small child just across from me trying to kick the seat in front of him. I hoped he wouldn't be on my flight the wait in departure was bad enough without having him sat behind me. Taking a deep breath I looked around once more, my eye passing the luminous signs with their nicotine coloured writing and a wide screen TV that was on silent but I my eyes froze when a young guy who was in his late 20's , who was tall about 5'11 inches height. A perfect body, rigged out with muscles like a ship with ropes, its limbs appearing to open out like a star around that fleece where there rises, in contrast to woman. Still, it has that amazing simile, "rigged out with muscles like a ship with ropes" which alone is worth an evening's awestruck contemplation, and the star, and the fleece. It may not be perfect, but it is still very, very good. Yes but the smile wasn't for me, it was Arpan yes but holding a girl whose face was sallow, it was true, with heavy beetled brows, and lips as thin as paper with a huge smile as a mile with all the teeth visible. Her watery blue eyes did nothing to her credit, only accentuating her potato nose and fair complexion. The heavy jowls that hung below her chin, creating a cave of sorts, drug down her mouth; the result ending up much like a slobbering living being. Her pasty cheeks were droopy, sagging down through all the wrinkles. And the hair? Say it isn't so! The oily grey tresses hung around her face, completing the picture of absolute despondency. The girl was Simran and it was Arpan's birthday and he wasn't going with the clients to any hill station. He was going with Simran to Goa to celebrate his birthday. They kissed each other on the Airport and were playing with each other and stood in a queue to gate No. 22 to board their flight. My face went slack, mouth slightly open, body unmoving and colour draining from my face as the eyes stared wide-eyed at something no one else can see. My eyes froze up to the point where I could hardly breathe. There was a sudden sigh; I opened my mouth to speak. Snap it shut. Gulp. The hot coffee tumbler which I was holding in my hand was left from my hands was all over me with the burnt body. Then with a little more success I said something when my dad asked what went wrong I said but it came out raspy, barely audible. I showed dad what I saw and my dad went in shock as well. He didn't say a word. The announcement made for our flight. I couldn't move my limbs, my dad escorted me from the chair and was feeling disoriented and the mind was buzzing which shook me inside out and I was shattered. I was shocked and fell in vain.

When I was one and twenty;

I heard my dad say;

Give crowns and pounds and guineas;

But not your heart away;

Give emeralds and rubies;

But never your heart away;

But my love went in vain;

And he made my life in pain.

After that day he didn't call me for many days and then after seven-days he called me up and asked what went wrong? I asked him not to call me again and just said I saw you at the Airport with Simran. And he didn't explain anything and kept down the phone.

"What the fucking hell was that"?? — I shouted and so did Ajit and Ishita.

"You never blasted him"?? — I asked this irritably. "Never said anything ever"? — Ajit added.

"NEVER EVER"!! Aisha put down her head down on the beach with her whiskey glass and there were tears rolling from her left ear and the right eye was just in an edge to fall out.

I wanted to hug Aisha and said I Love you and hug her. She felt like her heart had been ripped out. Suddenly there was an aura of grey around her. It was a mist that wouldn't rise. A state of depression that she couldn't see herself through. She felt a terrible weight on her shoulders. It was as if a giant boulder was laid on her and she couldn't straighten up or catch her breath entirely. A sinter sudden, deep pain in her heart was so bad, she felt like her whole world collapsed. She looked like death and she didn't care. Her eyes were puffy from crying because she couldn't stop crying for the last three hours. She was dehydrated, and sore. Sobs raked her body; no one should be able to cry that hard. She hadn't even cried ever I guess. Rejected, she wasn't wanted. It wasn't fair. It wasn't right. Now I have more respect for her. Now I love her more but I wanted to tell her how I was feeling about her but if I say this now she will take it otherwise.

We went back to Gwalior and four of us were now really good friends (yes including Ajit) :. We get along really nice now I have real good friends and my love of my life. She was my real Love and I think the only girl I could ever even think what I felt. Falling in love is just like going crazy. We get a new perspective or paradigm. Life seems always in budding-blooming; but heart breaks it is like booming-blasting (as I heard from Aisha and saw her). With the soft and sweet feeling of love there are negative feelings like fear of rejection, loosing are dearly attached. It is the duality of love. Scientifically it might only be adrenaline rush but emotionally it is something we all crave, no matter how wretched we are. Loving is losing (your ego, self-centeredness, even your weight sometimes).

Thankfully, some really have the patience and empathy to love others. (Like Aisha)

It is simply like a sweet and serene poem. And yes we do silly things in love. Love is like a pact made by two humans silently and secretly, like a chemical bond. It is like being frightened and elated at the same time. The fear comes from realising you have no choice but to love this person in all things and the elation comes from doing it.

I couldn't get my mind off her! When I see her, I smile at every little thing! Tingley belly! Dreams, smile when I think of her!

Everything about them seems perfect!

Forgive them for the little things that annoy!

It's like having a constant Anxiety attack!! :)

An equal mixture of pure ecstasy and pure pain

Pathetic and helpless.....but in a lovely way.

A few months after we returned from Puri, the 4 of us decided to go to Delhi to visit the weekend and have fun in the weekend. I wasn't in a state to go because I was coughing a lot from some a lot of days and had a slight fever and was feeling weak but I decided to go because Aisha was going and I cannot miss the chance. We reached Delhi on Saturday and after resting in the hotel for a while, four of us — Aisha, Ishita, Ajit and I started off. Four of us, we were roaming in Connaught Place. Ajit and Ishita went to Pica Delhi to book a table for four and they waited for us there because Aisha wanted to grab a bucket of COCOBERRY with her mangoes and kiwis. She took the bucket and took it like a six years old small little girl whose eyes were glittering when she had her Cocoberry and I was having my cigarette. Aisha was wearing a white sleeve top which had a back open with a sexiest pair of denim shorts and wore a brown belt which was making her more sexy and attractive. She has a unique sense of dressing. I was looking at her how she was enjoying her yogurt with her closed eyes like a little baby. Suddenly, she stopped when an average looking girl heighted about 5'2 inches and was wearing red specs and had an extremely sharp nose and a nose ring on it very fair and lips so wide that all her teeth were visible and I think I could count all of them who was hugging a guy who was about six feet tall, a perfect body, rigged out with muscles like a ship with ropes and his flawless olive skin accentuated her pecan shaped hazel eyes. The guy stopped in front of Aisha and his smile changed into Dismay and said "Hello, How are you"? And she said— "I am good!" And Aisha held my hand and started to walk. After a while when Aisha was quiet and not enjoying her Cocoberry I asked Aisha— "Who were they? "Your friends"?

Aisha replied— "They were Arpan and Simran"!!!!! (She is still walking)

"WHAT THE FUCK"???? And you didn't say a word"— I rushed behind Arpan and almost sprinted to bang his face down on the floor and in front of everywhere but Aisha held my hand and nodded her head for a NO!! I stopped but I wanted to.

"But why are you quiet"??? "It is his fault" — I replied.

"Varun what will happen if I fight, I don't want to fight because I don't want his face in front of my eyes and I don't want his voice to reach my ears. It is all over yes there will be the heartbreaking feeling will always with me on my dead bed. So no use because I don't want him in my life and even after my death."— She said and her tears rolled from her eyes.

"Aishhhhh. Wear your shades. You have a brighter future without him. Wear them you need it" — I said to her.

She hugged me tight and smiled and said —"Varun stay with me always and be with me I really need you, You are my best best friend, My friend forever."

And she took my heart away and made my day and my weak knees gave me strength and I could be strong and hugged her that day we boozed at Hard Rock Café at Saket and had a real good time but only Aisha was annoyed when I took a lot of time using the washroom.

We went back to Gwalior and my weakness grew and I took leave from office and stayed at home for few days. It had been raining for more than a week, so much rain it made everyday seemed so restless and gloomy. Aisha called and said she was coming up to see me. It was the third time she came up to see me that week. I carried her excuse of why she came so late in the night. It was raining and she looked fragile and weak, wearing not enough to keep her warm.

She said "Miss you". I just smiled at her and did not reply. We both were sitting in my room and not caring about who just passed by in the room whether it were my parents. We waited and waited; she looked at me innocently and smiled her. I know what she meant and expected the same from me. I understand how she must feel when she came so late in the night in this harsh rain. I felt guilt and wanted her to stay for the night. But reality struck again, I said to her coldly. "let me reach you till your home".

Tripping round the town

As the sun comes down

Flying with your friends

With the stars alive

Running on a high from the spirit inside

Taking on the world with an innocent smile

Something knocked me down

And I fell far to the ground

I lost it all in one night

Just wandering around

Break a few things say it wasn't easy

Let it all kick in, take you for a ride

Something knocked me down

And I fell far to the ground

That's when I got the shiver

That re-awoke my mind

You turned it all around

It only took your smile

Running on a high from the spirit inside

Taking on the world with an innocent smile

We were living in the same locality and four of us made us get along well. We eat dinner together, watch movies and sometimes go on trips. We were more like a family, but I didn't know I would end up falling in love with the only girl. We were walking from my room to the drawing room and then to the garage she was in front of me and I was right behind her. The rain had stopped but it could start any minute because the dark clouds were all over with no stars and moons which made it gloomy. I wanted to just take her in my arms with all my love but I did not and controlled with the constant pain in my stomach. There was a park nearby. She begged and said "Let's go to the park just for a while, please, you will feel good. I promise I will go home after this". With her begging, my heart softened, but I still put my annoyed face and walked in the park, I was just sitting on the benches and showed her I wanted to leave. I felt so sour inside; there was a stream of pain, flowing into my heart, the kind of pain I have never felt before. But all I can do was pretend I didn't care and said, "Can we go now"?

Two years ago, the doctor said I had Lung cancer because of excessive smoking, but I found early, so it was curable (that day at Hard Rock Café when Aisha was annoyed me for taking so much time in the bathroom was the first time I coughed with blood out and then I start losing weight and getting weak). Thinking that it was okay, I started living my normal life again, and even forgot about the disease. I didn't think of cancer again and didn't go back to the doctor. Until a month ago, my stomach was hurting for two weeks straight and the nightmare awakened me again. First, I thought the pain would go away, but it grew stronger until to a point that I couldn't take it anymore. I went back to the doctor and went under some tests and X-ray. The picture came out and there was a big black spot, which proved the truth I did not want to believe. It was the most glittering part of my life, but it was coming to an end. I wanted myself and the people around me to go through the least pain possible, so I decided not to tell Aisha. But Ishita, Ajit and my parents knew.

We were just standing outside her main gate, waiting, losing our last moments in silence. I held my tears and said to her "Take care of yourself, eat well and take real good care". She didn't talk just nodded lightly and said to me "Get well soon and we will party together, only you and me this time". I felt what she meant. She started moving inside her house. Finally, I couldn't hold my sorrow and the twist in my heart any longer. I wanted to chase her because I knew, this would be the last time I see her. I wanted to tell her that how much I loved her, I wanted to tell her to stay, I wanted to tell her so much but god hasn't given me enough time to me. I had just few days in my life and I felt cursed. Warm tears kept falling down my face, blended with the cold rain drops. I was cold not because of the rain. I was cold inside.

She left, and I didn't get anymore of her phone calls even until today. I know she didn't see my tears because they were washed away by the rain. I left with regrets of not telling Aisha about my first and only love. But I am not Varun, I am the girl Aisha, using my memory, and his diary I found after two months since he left, writing down these last words.